Into the Ruins

Issue 3
Fall 2016

Published November 2016 by Figuration Press
Portland, Oregon

Into the Ruins is a project and publication of Figuration Press,
a small publication house focused on alternate visions of the future
and alternate ways of understanding the world,
particularly in ecological contexts.

intotheruins.com

figurationpress.com

ISBN 13: 978-0-9978656-1-5
ISBN 10: 0-9978656-1-X

Editor's Note:
Other than 2008, has there been a year in recent memory
that has felt more like an inflection point for the United States?
What will 2017 bring?

Comments and feedback always welcome at editor@intotheruins.com
Comments for authors will be forwarded.

Issue 3
Fall 2016

TABLE OF CONTENTS

PREAMBLE

STORIES

REVIEWS

PREAMBLE

DISQUIETING VISTAS

BY JOEL CARIS

In *The Geography of Childhood*'s opening essay, "A Child's Sense of Wildness," Gary Paul Nabhan makes the observation that children tend to focus on small, micro elements of the natural world. Exploring the outdoors with his own children, he notices as they pay their attention to "the darting of water striders [and] the shapes of creek-washed stones," and "scramble up slopes to inspect petroglyphs and down arroyos to enter keyhole canyons." Meanwhile, he observes how adults pay their attention to the macro elements of the natural world, "scanning the land for picturesque panoramas and scenic overlooks," the sort of scenery we take long hikes to come upon. Reading it some years back, I found it a fascinating observation that rang true, sticking with me as one of those remembered insights that has many times helped me make sense of the world.

As it happens, that insight has helped me once again. One of my challenges in expecting a harsh future lies in my tendency to think of these possible futures in broad, macro terms—as scenery that's stunning in all the wrong ways. I see the possibilities of economic trouble, geopolitical flare ups, destructive wars, political and social upheaval, domestic insurgencies, and so much more. I imagine how it might feel to be caught in the cracks of a clash between world powers, to not be able to provide for myself or the people I love, to be at the mercy of cascading political chaos or vindictive social reprisals. Since I can't truly know the future in advance, my imaginings of its trouble sometimes take the form of a certain suffocating foreboding—a general, dark malaise.

It's a change of pace from other times of my life, particularly when I was young. At that point, I believed in the beneficence of progress and the ability of the onward march of time to provide me a better life. It's not that that's what always happened, it's just that I believed more often than not that it would, even if the current moment suggested the opposite. I considered such dispiriting moments a setback, and little more.

I still sometimes feel that way. It's an odd discordance that I often expect our collective future to be harsh but still hold out hopes that my own future will be an improvement: stronger and better interpersonal relationships, more satisfying work, modest but comfortable financial success, a sense of contributing to the world in a positive way—and perhaps even having a super awesome weekend. It's not that I think this is crazy or deluded; such a divergence of fortunes is entirely possible and happens regularly. But I don't know that there's any particular reason I should expect to escape the negative impacts of the hard times ahead. A crumbling economy, dark political undercurrents, social upheaval, a major war, and an upending of the current socioeconomic order all threaten to impact me. I'm not the most vulnerable person in this country, but I'm far from the least. I would place myself somewhere solid in the middle, and such troubles may have a very large impact on my life indeed.

Therefore, the macro picture is a dangerous one for me—or so I believe. The stunning vistas are disquieting, the picturesque panoramas foreboding. They threaten my comfort and stability. And so sometimes, when I feel as though these panoramas are coming into a disturbing focus, a darkness falls over me. This happened to me recently, as the American election devolved into a toxic stew of bitter anger and betrayal—furious conflicts in interest, values, and world-views—and I found myself caught in a wary sympathy for many voters on both sides, as well as glimpsing the beginning of a too-close upheaval that I could all-too-easily imagine cleaving my life into pieces. From there, I began to expand my view, moving from one dark element of the overlook in front of me to several others, taking a hard look at the chaotic outline of geopolitical reality, the simmering anger against the establishment, the crushing opioid epidemic ripping through this country, particularly within our heartland, and the utter discord and disconnect between the significant chunk of this country that is well off enough to feel an investment in the continuation of some version of the status quo and those who have been so utterly crushed by the economic and political dysfunction in America that, their backs against the wall, they would consider most anyone or any course of action that might bring acknowledgment of their plight and change in the organizing principles of this country.

It took me a few weeks to extract myself from that miasma. I will never claim not to have my bad habits, and I am skilled—at times, anyway—at backing myself into a single-view corner and drilling down into one particular, nagging sensation. I had to make a few messes, so to speak, and make myself crazy for awhile before I finally began backing away from the self-sabotage and recognizing my need to seed some different perspectives and create other foci. Granted, it's not that I felt my concerns were unfounded or unrealistic, but that it did me little good to maintain such a laser focus on a troubled outcome I had little control over. I could not change that vista in front of me, after all—or if I could, it would be only the smallest chiseling of a tiny point upon one of its peaks, so small that it could never be seen from any sort of encompassing vantage point.

What was missing? Reflecting on it, I believe it was the micro. So caught in my macro views, I ignored the multitude of micro views also available to me. That doesn't mean that all those views are enjoyable. Some are dark and foreboding themselves, of course, but the detail provides variety. It means that there are joyful views mixed in with those dark ones, even when they exist within the darker vista. It means, as well, that the dark views that remain can still take on a certain palatability, rooted in the small intimacies of human interaction, far too often destructive but just as or more often kind and heartening. We are all too quick to judge and create sweeping categorizations—all of us, across all ideologies—and yet I've watched people I admire as well as those I very much don't act with a kindness and neighborliness toward those in their lives, even when they are humans of strikingly different color (literal and otherwise).

In addition to the complicated tendency of human kindness and human division, there is the encompassing beauty and alleviating grace of the natural world. I have written before of its savings—of shattered ice on river rock, the singing of frogs, the sudden nighttime yips and howls of coyotes—and even at a time of such national upheaval, it provides its daily blessings and respites. Of late, that has taken the form of crows hopping around our backyard, poking at the grass and ground beneath with their beaks, no doubt searching out treats and sustenance, their demeanor steady, alert, and by all appearances happy. It takes, as well, the form of autumn-crazed squirrels, darting back and forth and at times jumping wildly, through no obvious prevarication, digging at various intervals, ransacking bushes, chasing each other in wild abandon, and searching manic for their winter keep. I've watched all of this with a steady amusement and low-key delight, thankful each day for these seasonal set pieces.

I walked this city recently on a gorgeous fall day, the sky a perfect blue and the air holding a hint of chill, just enough removed from the cold for me to be in only a t-shirt. Like so many others, I love the falling leaves this time of year, and I love especially a cool and windy day in which those dry and brittle leaves swirl across the roads and sidewalks, their skitter such a distinct and seasonal sound. Wrapped within these sensations, the natural world defined so sharp around me, I couldn't help but feel happy and satisfied. I couldn't help but be lifted by the life and natural cycles so evident with every step. It is an interesting thing that we humans can create such pain and suffering while being just as much a part of the natural world that brings such joy and celebration. And it sometimes is a hard thing to gain perspective on our own complex but small corner of the natural world. It is hard to step back and see that something that seems so big is actually so very small within its broader context.

It's in this knowledge that I take my solace and it's in my own fictional explorations of this future over the past several weeks—my having discovered a renewed focus of late for writing stories and exploring characters—that I have, in part, regained my perspective. For while the broad sweeps of our future may look dark, it's through the close examination of the individual lives involved that we can best begin to see the day-to-day experiences that expose and illuminate our world's virtues. The stories that unwind themselves in the following pages, at their best, do the same to help to provide that perspective. The machinations of our time can be disturbing indeed, and I find no dishonesty in a sense of foreboding. But our time is small—just the barest piece of something unimaginably large—and glimpsing a possible future, and all the ways that humans continue within it, can help us remember that ours is not an end but just one small detail within an impossibly complex tapestry. In that context, our macro is time's micro, and however dark our macro may appear, it is only one of an uncountable number of micros of all shapes and sizes: joyous and devastating, mundane and exciting, meditative and cruel, and so much between and beyond.

Granted, that is a perspective we don't come to easily as humans, and it is just as helpful and honest to come back to the micros of our own lives within the macros of the broader sweep of history. Yes, we live in a tumultuous moment and we don't know where it will take us, or whether our destinations will be as good or bad as we expect. But we do know that there will be joy along the way, even if there is despair, indifference, and so much more, as well. The crows and squirrels will be there, poking around in the backyard. The coyotes—well, they're not going anywhere, and I imagine they'll be filling the night air with their cries and exultations for a long time indeed. Ice will still shatter against rock, leaves will drop in the fall, and the autumn winds will swirl them across the landscape, whether that be concrete or otherwise. Soils will continue to be made up of incomprehensibly large and complex communities of dead, dying, and living creatures. Ducks will still take joy in bodies of water large and small, and somewhere they will wait patiently for their turn in the nearest kiddie pool—at least, so long as ducks are kept by humans and plastic kiddie pools remain to make convenient artificial ponds.

And at some point in the far future—no matter how this current political climate unfolds, or what geopolitical convulsions take place, or whose economy collapses and whose thrives—an old man, somewhere, will plant a garden and bring new life to abused soil; a group of friends will dance in celebration of the changing seasons; a woman will fight against the exploitation of herself and others. At some farther point, humans will no longer be here at all, but the earth's complex interweaving of innumerable lives will continue on apace for an impossibly long time before eventually drawing to a close.

In the meantime, there is so much to be experienced here, good and bad. Plenty will be familiar within the context of today's human arrangements and the vast majority more will be some degree of alien to those of us alive now. There is a fascinating amount of human experience yet to play out on this planet, and each of us will only get the most microscopic portion of that experience. But en-compassed within that tiny stretch—our blessed, exultant lives—will be a vast ar-ray of experiences that will test our limits and expose our many truths, even when those truths contradict each other. The macro sweep of our own lives can only exist moment by moment, each of those their own micros, building ultimately to a sweeping landscape the full extent of which we can only discover at death. At times it will appear dark and foreboding, at other times bright and joyous. And in the end, it can only be all of these things. It's in our hard-fought perspective, our recognition of the full breadth of experience still awaiting us, that we can place the uncertainty of this time in its proper place and recognize that the world will continually grace us in its own particular way, regardless of our hopes, fears, or expectations.

— Portland, Oregon
October 29, 2016

Litterfall

Conversations on peak oil, decline, living with less, and an honest consideration of the hope and hard times ahead of us.

ANNOUNCEMENT

In August of this year, your friendly *Into the Ruins* editor launched a new blog on the Figuration Press website called Litterfall. As I wrote in the introductory post, the purpose of the blog is to host a weekly conversation on peak oil, decline, living with less, connection to the natural world, and an honest considering of the hope and hard times ahead of us. Since I wrote that first post, I've published quite a few more, updating each Monday evening, and have dived into subjects of empire, resource and energy depletion, the rising costs of our ways of living, the decline of our ecosystem's resiliency, the problems with our organizing economic principles, and more. I have started to introduce the concept of "Closed System Economics," which I will be exploring in greater detail in the months to come. And I have been unveiling a deindustrial science fiction story of my own, introducing a near-future setting and characters I will be exploring in greater detail in at least one future issue of this magazine.

While a number of the initial posts have focused on laying out the troubles facing us and communicating my own particular world view, coming posts will be talking about some of the ways we may yet respond to our predicaments in an effort to make the future better than it might otherwise be. I hope for Litterfall to be a place of consideration where we can have a conversation about how to best change our ways of living. If you haven't already, consider visiting, reading a post or two, and adding to the conversation. As noted, I'll be updating every week on Monday evenings.

I hope to see you there.

To read and follow Litterfall, please visit:

figurationpress.com/litterfall

Into the Ruins is published quarterly by Figuration Press. We publish deindustrial science fiction that explores a future defined by natural limits, energy and resource depletion, industrial decline, climate change, and other consequences stemming from the reckless and shortsighted exploitation of our planet, as well as the ways that humans will adapt, survive, live, die, and thrive within this future.

One year, four issue subscriptions to *Into the Ruins* are $39. You can subscribe by visiting intotheruins.com or by mailing a check made out to Figuration Press to:

Figuration Press / 3515 SE Clinton Street / Portland, OR 97202

To submit your work for publication, please visit intotheruins.com/submissions or email submissions@intotheruins.com.

All issues of *Into the Ruins* are printed on paper, first and foremost. Electronic versions will be made available as high quality PDF downloads. Please visit our website for more information. The opinions expressed by the authors do not necessarily reflect the opinions of Figuration Press or *Into the Ruins*. Except those expressed by Joel Caris, since this is a sole proprietorship. That said, all opinions are subject to (and commonly do) change, for despite the Editor's occasional actions suggesting the contrary, it turns out he does not know everything and the world often still surprises him.

ADVERTISEMENT

EDITOR-IN-CHIEF
JOEL CARIS

ASSOCIATE EDITOR
SHANE WILSON

DESIGNER
JOEL CARIS

WITH THANKS TO
SHANE WILSON
JOHN MICHAEL GREER
OUR SUBSCRIBERS

SPECIAL THANKS TO
KATE O'NEILL

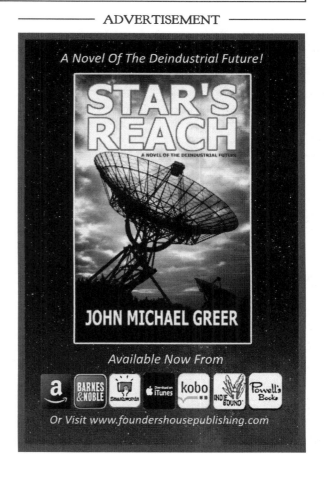

CONTRIBUTORS

Although born in New Jersey, **CATHERINE MCGUIRE** has been steeped in the beauties of the Northwest for over thirty years. She has short stories coming out in the anthology *Merigan Tales* and in the science fiction and fantasy magazine *Mythic*, as well as a deindustrial science fiction novel, *Lifeline*, coming this winter from Founders House Publishing. For those who like poetry, she now has a full-length book of poems, *Elegy for the 21st Century* (FutureCycle Press). See cathymcguire.com for the latest.

JOEL CARIS is a gardener and homesteader, occasional farmer, passionate advocate for local and community food systems, sporadic writer, voracious reader, sometimes prone to distraction and too attendant to detail, a little bit crazy, a cynical optimist, and both deeply empathetic toward and frustrated with humanity. He is your friendly local editor and publisher. As a reader of this journal and perhaps his blog, Litterfall, he hopes you don't too easily tire of his voice and perspective. He lives in Oregon with an amazing, endlessly patient woman who somehow makes him a better person every single damn day. You can catch up on his weekly blog at figurationpress.com/litterfall

JASON HEPPENSTALL is an ex-journalist, newspaper editor and energy analyst from the English Midlands. After spending years travelling around the world and living in Denmark and Spain he now resides with his family in Cornwall, UK, where he sustainably manages a damp woodland and grows mushrooms. Describing himself as an optimistic realist, Jason writes about facing up to our future on his blog, *22 Billion Energy Slaves*, and released a book in 2015 called *The Path to Odin's Lake* about the spiritual aspect of the Long Descent.

JUSTIN PATRICK MOORE, KE8COY, is a writer, radio hobbyist and student of the Mysteries. His work has been published in *AntenneX*, *Flurb* and *Abraxas: International Journal of Esoteric Studies*. The various flavors of his writings can be sampled at sothismedias.com. He was on the airwaves for over ten years at community station WAIF 88.3 FM on the shows *Art Damage* and *On the Way to the Peak of Normal*. After being off the air he found he still had the radio bug and acquired a ham license that is providing a new realm of growth and exploration. Justin and his wife Audrey make their home in Cincinnati, the Queen of the West.

W. JACK SAVAGE is a retired broadcaster and educator. He is the author of seven books, including *Imagination: The Art of W. Jack Savage* (wjacksavage.com). To date, more than fifty of Jack's short stories and over seven hundred of his paintings and drawings have been published worldwide. Jack and his wife Kathy live in Monrovia, California. Jack is again responsible for this issue's cover art.

IAN O'REILLY is an alternate-reality version of a freelance writer from the UK. One Ian studied Anthropology and Philosophy, and has worked in bookshops and for international publishers. The other Ian has an interest in direct democracy, sustainability, and mental health. Both are interested in stories about hope and adventure, zap-guns and monsters. One of Ian's work has appeared in *Solar Punk Press*, *Third Flatiron*, and *Stories of Imagination*. We are assured that this is not even their final form.

Born in the gritty Navy town of Bremerton, Washington and raised in the south Seattle suburbs, **JOHN MICHAEL GREER** started writing about as soon as he could hold a pencil. He is the author of more than forty nonfiction books and four novels, including the deindustrial novel *Star's Reach*, as well as the weekly blog "The Archdruid Report," and has edited four volumes of the *After Oil* series of deindustrial SF anthologies. These days he lives in Cumberland, Maryland, an old red brick mill town in the north central Appalachians, with his wife Sara.

RACHEL WHITE works in youth services at a public library and sporadically writes poetry and fiction. Her most recent short story was published in the *After Oil 2* anthology. When she is not immersed in books, she enjoys hiking and exploring the natural world. She is interested in stories of many kinds, especially myth and folklore, as they relate to the unraveling of the industrial age. A native of Delaware, she now lives in Washington, DC.

MATTHEW GRIFFITHS is a New Zealand engineer and environmental planner working in environmental protection who lives in Brisbane, Australia with his wife and two children. He loves reading and writing, especially about his main interests: ecological sustainability, Tibet and China. He also enjoys travelling and speaking other languages badly and at other times plays guitar with more enthusiasm than skill. He writes regularly at: eastwestfuturestories.blogspot.com.au

Letters to the Editor

Dear Editor,

I want to share a story regarding a conversation I had a few weeks ago. I have a friend whom I call regularly (he lives quite far away). My friend is the poster child for a believer in progress. He works in a high-tech job and he is convinced that tomorrow will be better than today because of technology. No amount of arguing from my side can change his mind or opinion.

During a recent conversation, we started discussing the "green" efforts being made by companies like Apple and Tesla. I quipped that no matter how "green" a company is, if they still have a growth imperative they cannot be sustainable. I mentioned how all these high technology products rely on scarcer and scarcer resources to which my friend replied with finality that the earth is full of metals, that the core is metal, and that we would find a way to gain access to the deeper metals in due time. This colossal thought-stopper left me speechless.

Other highlights from the conversation include how humanity would achieve immortality before the next millennium and how it was only once a company became profitable by doing the wrong thing (planned obsolesce, wasteful packaging, etc.) that they could start focusing their efforts on doing the right thing.

The tricky thing for me is that sometimes his assertions are so insidiously plausible. I can see how easily and comforting it is to extrapolate the best parts of the past few decades onto the future, towards our manifest destiny as the rulers of the universe.

I doubt that I will be able to change my friend's mind, but I would settle for sowing a few doubts in his certainty. My efforts so far have failed since any evidence that I present gets turned into fodder for showing how using technology will be different this time around.

I was wondering if any of my fellow readers here could offer advice for how to deal with devout believers in progress?

Regards,

Marcu Knoesen
Melbourne, Australia

Editor's Note: On September 1st, I posted a blog post on the Into the Ruins website asking readers what unmentionable and ignored issue they would like to see an American presidential candidate center their campaign upon, keeping in mind the themes of this journal. I asked that, so far as possible, they not mention any of the 2016 candidates (almost successful!) but instead focus on issues that, for the large part, are ignored in this country. Following are some of the responses I received.

Dear Editor,

You may already know that the Federal highway system was built in response to fears that railroads make excellent targets for aerial bombardment, hence are more vulnerable than an open road system for for internal military logistics transport.

Also, you may already be aware that the railroads were initially built by for-profit companies that strove with all their might to bar competitors or gobble up small fry in a shark-tank feeding frenzy fashion. The Grange used to have its own lines in response to fat-cat railroad men gouging farmers by unregulated rises in the price of produce transit. So the fat-cats combined to drive the Grange out of business and leave the field free for them to gouge at will. This helped ruin railroads for everyone by making them uneconomical for use both coming and going.

However, the dendritic, internet-server clusternet model of transport helps to solve both these problems. If a local group of food producers could build a local narrow-gauge rail system that runs from outlying farms into the nearest market town, that would be the start of a distributed network of slow-rail transit that could eventually be tied together by a high-speed spinal cord of passenger rail.

Local co-operative ownership of the rail service would provide part-time work for a whole suite of technical, mechanical, and maintenance jobs that could be filled by local high-school-age youths. Federal funds for job creation could be one source of start-up or continuation funds. Such a group might be able to attract federal funds for their project by linking farms to military bases for use in emergency disaster response. Pork barrel funds might be easier to siphon off from weapons manufacture if a logistics supply angle was stressed in the proposal. Narrow gauge rail does not make a very cost-effective bombing target because it is easily repaired (even temporarily running on reclaimed wood for rails) for slow-going and lightly-freighted cars.

Intermediate uses of the narrow-gauge local nets could be integrated into local economies by renting cargo space on the local food train to Fed Ex, the U.S. Postal Service and one paying passenger car for school kids, commuters, and tourists. They could also be used to transport spoiled food waste to a composting center beside the mini-hub centrally positioned among the farms. Eventually, they could also transport loads of chicken straw and humanure from town out to the composting fields.

This is the idea I used in "Coyote Year" [Issue #1 of *Into the Ruins*] for transporting the heroes up to Geartown.

G.Kay Bishop
Durham, North Carolina

Dear Editor,

I kept hoping that Trump would eventually synthesize a coherent philosophy or viewpoint or program that recognized the extreme dysfunction of classic economic models today. I wish I could make him coax out some broader principles, which I would summarize as follows:

1. Economic policies that primarily promote or encourage growth and increased productivity are misguided in today's world, and destined to fail.

2. Globalization causes extreme wealth concentration in those who own capital assets, which in turn destabilizes economies, polities and societies.

3. Prosperity and stability can return only in those Western nations which focus on the relocalization of economic activity, particularly the local creation of local private sector jobs.

4. Tariffs and well-controlled borders are always characteristic of the world's strongest economies, and ought to be characteristic of America.

5. America has a fortuitous and rare—perhaps unique—combination of natural resources (particularly arable land) that enable it to be economically self-sufficient if it chooses to be.

6. Social policies that give able-bodied adults something for nothing on a continuing basis are ruinously immoral and dangerously destabilizing, and must be phased out humanely, over the course of 10 or 15 or 20 years.

7. The lives of Americans of future generations can be more interesting, more satisfying and more fulfilling than (most of) our lives today, but only if we learn to rely on our ourselves, on our families, on our friends, on our neighbors and on our fellow citizens, and not on government at any level.

I don't know of any politician in America today who would get behind all seven of these points, but I honestly believe that if any national politician would adopt them and hammer on them, he or she would be unbeatable. This belief may be irrational.

Bart Hillyer
Mascoutah, Illinois

Dear Editor,

I think, based on Hillary Clinton's famous "We came, we saw, he died" video regarding Muammar Gaddafi, that our real need for the largest military on the planet needs to be questioned. Not only did that interview disturb me at a gut level, it also made me absolutely certain that I would never allow my children to be conscripted into the military. She was not just proud, but sadistically gleeful about the man being killed.

We sell nearly twice as many weapons as Russia, our nearest competitor in arms sales, and five times as much as the number three country, China.

We have over 600 foreign military bases, or 800 or 1,400—it depends on what you define a base as. No other country is close, none over 100 at any rate. And the US has never allowed a foreign base in our country—imagine that.

Over $600,000,000,000 yearly spent on "defending America." This does not include the CIA, NSA, DHS or other federal entities involved in spying or subversion, nor does it include "black budget" expenditures, "program prepayments" given to the military suppliers and many other hidden budget items. China spends a little over $200,000,000,000 and Russia well under $100,000,000,000 for their "defense." I don't think it takes a genius to figure out who Russia and China might feel threatened by.

We routinely violate other country's airspaces, bomb their citizens and sail into their territorial waters. Yet we would deem it a violent provocation if something similar were to be done to America.

Our federal debt is approaching $20 trillion, and that is the 'offishul' number—not taking into account empty social security funding and many other items. We routinely run annual budget deficits of half a trillion dollars these last couple of years.

In short, this cannot go on because we are consuming our own tail via this debt.

So my question is, what *should* we do with our military in lieu of "protecting" the entire planet from the latest evil ginned up by the media? What do we really need to be secure within our borders? What could we do with just a portion of what we spend on our military adventures?

Because, let's face it: nobody else is close to us in terms of adventurism or expenditures.

And because, somehow, other countries have equivalent standards of living without these massive military expenses . . .

J. Shamburger
Deep Woods of East Texas

Dear Editor,

One unmentionable (perhaps even unseen) issue is that our society has moved faster and faster, like an out of control assembly line, and we are close to or beyond our capabilities to cope. The current pace of life is so much faster than even 20 years ago, and yet we never mention that as a root cause of 1) anxiety, 2) depression, 3) hostility toward others, 4) inability to grasp and think through the complexities of society. (Oh, yes—and substance abuse.) I realize that eventually every generation says "it's moving too fast," but that's probably true—part of our "progress" since the Industrial Revolution is pushing to do everything faster. Have we hit "peak speed"?

When I think about the people working two or three jobs, I wonder how any of them can take enough time to investigate the claims of any candidate, let alone the serious new challenges we have in peak oil, climate change and natural resource depletion. Studies show people are losing their ability to read and digest long articles. People can't keep from checking their tweets and emails, so they can't hold a decent conversation (and some are required by bosses to be always on-call). So how will those on different political sides dialogue to find compromise? And some of the best non-profits I've worked for have, in the past 10 years, lost significant numbers of volunteers because those people are now overworked and can't take extra time. And of course, people are getting sick from this level of hurry and constant vigilance—I haven't checked to see if anyone is measuring, but the added stress has got to be costing millions in medical bills. And yet nowhere do I see any real calls to slow down, to push back against the relentless "efficiency campaigns" that push workers to work harder, faster, more mindlessly.

The current "solution" seems to be to make it "faster and more efficient" to do certain things (like buying, primarily), but have we really looked at what we've chosen to sideline as we move toward more electronic communication, more complex (and vulnerable) "cloud" data, and "just in time" supply lines? What if the more sane response was to start calling for slower workplaces, less instant responses, more time together just chatting? Maybe even go back to one day "of rest" where all the stores are closed?? (Doesn't have to be Sunday.) Some of this is pushing back against the vampire rich who want to suck us dry. But if we don't acknowledge this as a root problem, the chances of a solution are slim.

Cathy McGuire
Sweet Home, Oregon

Dear Editor,

You wish to know a subject that the political candidates should discuss? Colleges. In particular, the lie that spending $100,000 will set you up for life in a cushy, well paying job. Okay, maybe "lie" is too strong. Perhaps "misleading"?

It is interesting that if you remind people that college was once only for the "rich," they immediately demand that everyone should have access. Well, everyone did have access, if you had the money. We the common folk had trade schools. When I was in high school they had "Vocational Tech" classes to get kids started on a career path. No longer. We need to bring those back, and not just the favorites like auto shop. We should be hosting introductions into as many trade crafts as possible. Plumbing, Electrical, Carpentry, and the myriad sub sets, such as high voltage electrical, low voltage electrical, masonry, solar/wind power, appliance repair, etc. It should not take a college degree to be a CPA, small business bookkeeper, or landscaper.

What most people are missing out

on is that quite often, in-demand blue collar jobs are so under staffed that they can command better incomes than some careers requiring college degrees! We have burdened our children with huge amounts of debt which will take most of their lifetime to pay off with no hope of reprieve even if they end up in bankruptcy. All for the sake of chasing easy money.

Time for a discussion.

Terrence M.
Portland, Oregon

Dear Editor,

Jay [Cumming]'s story ["Time's Ark," Issue #2, Summer 2016] was particularly interesting to me as it indirectly touched upon one of the unmentionables I've been considering. Namely, how will the conflict between the rich and powerful (and their fellow travelers) and the rest of us play out as the inevitable and various "peaks" begin to bite and affect the economics underlying the current balance of power. (I speak metaphorically.)

The aspects explored in the off-centre media and blogosphere are usually that of the widening gap between the rich, really rich, and the rest of us, and the negative social effects that may occur. At one extreme the more radical preppers fully expect our police, armed forces, and the odd war band to turn on us while at the other end of the spectrum the green techies expect to see capitalism with a human face shine the light from their entrenched hill. Many of our current stories seem to be about small groups, usually families, or communities and their adaptations to their changing world and they are very useful in raising my awareness and suggesting ways we will adapt.

I'm interested in how the western developed democracies (metaphoric again) will seek to use all the state institutions, media, and the rule of law to stave off perceived threats to their vision of how the world should be. Already in some countries, to be in political opposition to a ruling party is to end up in court.

Its not impossible that they might choose otherwise and only take one step back for every two forward taken.

Spengler and Toynbee pointed the way here but suffer from their place in time. Or is it hubris to think it's different for our time?

If anyone knows of such stories, I'd appreciate to hear of them. Thanks.

Dennis Brown
Emu Downs, Australia

Dear Editor,

Of all the problems and perils of our current time and place in history, one speaks closely to my heart.

I grew up on the ocean, and I saw first hand how we change it by dumping uncountable garbage onto beaches all over the world every day of the year. But that's not what I want to talk about. I'm not here to tell everyone that if you pick up every single piece of trash on a beach, it will be covered with the same amount of litter by morning (we did it anyway every year).

No, what I'm here to talk about is a different pollutant destroying our oceans: carbon dioxide. Humans have released so much carbon into the air that it has changed the pH of the oceans, making them measurably more acidic. By now everyone has heard of climate change, and most people have chosen a side. I encourage everyone to go back to the data and look again, because we need an honest appraisal of where we are as a species. As we acidify the ocean, we make it inhospitable to algae, mollusks, and fish, everything that relies on calcium structures in their body. Simultaneously, we create conditions that promote the growth of jellyfish.

As our world population speeds past seven billion and heads for eight billion, we destroy our fisheries (rising CO_2 is one of many things we do to destroy ocean ecosystems and kill fisheries), meanwhile fish is a staple food for humanity.

The reason I think ocean acidification is important is first, I love the ocean and it has provided for me my whole life. Second, it is a source of sustenance for the whole world, not just me. Finally, ocean acidification is a huge consequence of climate change that is never addressed. While governments continue to pay lip service to treaties and accords to reduce emissions, CO_2 keeps relentlessly rising,

and geoengineering is now being invoked as a possible solution. But if we geoengineer the planet to stay cool while we continue to spew carbon pollution, we throw the oceans under the bus, because geoengineering does nothing to restore the pH of the ocean and it gives everyone a free pass to keep spewing carbon and keep turning the ocean into a dead zone.

I don't seriously expect any politicians to mention the acidifying ocean. They have nothing to gain by solving these problems. We all know that politicians will continue to support the popular delusion that a bourgeois over-consumptive lifestyle is not only OK, it's something to be worshiped, valued, and envied.

But maybe, if enough of us pions make it a priority of our own, we can make the change ourselves, because we already know nobody in Washington cares about our grandkids. Oh wait, it's the new millennium, I mean our kids. Oh wait. It's 2016. The climate is changing right now, and Washington couldn't care less about any of us.

Sincerely,

Jessi Thompson
Spring Grove, Illinois

Dear Readers,

Every issue, we look for a set of compelling letters to the editor to spark thought and debate, consideration of the future ahead of us, and different ways that fiction might portray it. This section offers the opportunity for our readers to bring in their own thoughts and opinions, to play off the stories and editorial content of previous issues, and to help advance the conversation about what kind of future we're likely to get versus what kind of future our society most expects.

While one of the core ideas behind *Into the Ruins* is that the future our society expects is not likely the one we'll get, just what our future looks like is unknowable in advance and still open to a galaxy of possibilities. What role might alternative energy technologies play? What level of energy use is actually possible on a long-term basis? Which paths not taken may be reexamined and which will continue to be ignored? How will our degraded ecosystems impact our future? What collective choices will we make? When will vindictiveness win out, and when will kindness and compassion carry the day instead?

The stories in the following pages —and in the past two issues—make their own small attempts to answer these questions. Now we ask you, the reader, to react to those attempts. Are they realistic, or do you see a fatal flaw? In what ways do you think they get the future right and in what ways do you suspect they get it wrong? What kind of stories would you like to see, which issues tackled, which untraveled paths discovered anew?

This is your opportunity to join the conversation and to even help guide it. There are so many stories out there, and one or more may already be lurking in your own head. Perhaps you're not a writer; that's fine, you don't have to author the story yourself. But let those thoughts and insights out into the world and maybe you'll inspire a future story or begin a chain of thought and imagination within an author's head that concludes with the next great work of deindustrial science fiction. The letters page is a place to explore, debate, argue, praise, and inspire. Add your voice and bring a new dimension to the conversation.

Joel Caris, Editor
Portland, Oregon

Into the Ruins *welcomes letters to the editor from our readers. We encourage thoughtful commentary on the contents of this issue, the themes of the magazine, and humanity's collective future. Readers may email their letters to editor@intotheruins.com or mail to:*

Figuration Press
3515 SE Clinton Street
Portland, OR 97202

Please include your full name, city and state, and an email or phone number. Only your name and location will be printed with any accepted letter.

STORIES

THE FIFTH GARDEN
BY JASON HEPPENSTALL

The pueblo lay in the dun-coloured landscape, low and dusty and faded. A few high rises stood sentinel on its outskirts, bereft of all but their concrete frames and a patina of faded other-era graffiti. There was nothing remarkable about the place; it was just like any other.

The sun had slid behind the distant sierra and the earth was aching out its heat when the old man came to a halt on the road. Thinking he had heard something, he stopped and listened. There it was again. He laid down the handles of the cart on the cracked and potholed road and tried to ascertain the direction of the sound. The frog croaked once more. It seemed to be coming from a ditch beside the road. Frogs don't live in the dust, reasoned the old man, who for the last hundred miles and the last hundred days hadn't encountered so much as a puddle. This had to be a sign. He looked for others. A full moon was rising over the pueblo, which twinkled in the evening with its dim electric lights. The frog croaked once more. This place felt right.

The old man picked up the handles of his rickshaw and began to move again. Standing sharp against the yellow pink sky was an old petrol station. Its canopy was reduced to flaps of brittle plastic hanging forlornly over a concrete pad, and at its centre stood two rusting pumps. Pausing at the edge of the concrete the old man fumbled in a pouch and removed two rods. Perhaps it was too dark now, perhaps not, but in any case the rods cared not for the human requirement of light. He held them and walked slowly across the forecourt, focusing his attention and his intent as he went. He had only walked a few paces when there came a sudden movement of the rods. *That was a strong one*, thought the old man. He reset them and approached the spot from another direction. Again, the rods swung together and stayed there. The old man smiled.

That night, reclining on the rickshaw as he gazed up at the sky, the third and final sign displayed itself. The shooting star was not a flash-in-the-pan one. Instead it traversed the entire celestial dome. It went from north to south and seemed to leave an effervescent trail in its wake. *It's a sure thing*, thought the old man excitedly. *I've found the Fifth Garden*. As the night closed in, the howls and yaps of wild dogs in the nearby hills lulled the old man to sleep.

In the morning the old man rose with the sun, as he always did. He walked over to the ditch where he had heard the frog and got down on his hands and knees. The concrete drainage ditch was choked with the usual mess of plastic bottles and metal cans hidden amongst the dry stalks of dead reeds. He pulled them aside with his hands, plunging his fingers into the dust and dirt in search of moisture. A sulphurous earthy smell arose as he dug and when he pulled out his hand from the ditch, moist black mud dripped from his fingers onto the parched land. It stank of effluent and chemicals and decay, but it was good enough for the old man.

He went back to the spot on the forecourt and stood staring at it. *How thick would the concrete be? A foot, perhaps even two.* Whatever the thickness, it mattered not to the old man, who possessed nothing in this world but a few tools and endless patience. From a carpetbag on the rickshaw he took out a well-used lump hammer and a chisel and then he sat down on the concrete floor and began to chip away. This would be his last Garden, he knew that in his bones. Whether he would be permitted the chance to finish it would be God's will. The great beyond beckoned and the old man would be happy to return after this life of service.

It was three days before the people in the pueblo noticed him. The north road was not often used, but a traveller returning from a trip to the city noticed him as he was passing by. It wasn't long before the new arrival became the topic of conversation in the bar. "There's a crazy old koot digging for oil at the old petrol station on the autovia," they laughed. The next day one of those in the bar went out to have a look for himself. Alfonso was a stout man, and he was also the main butcher in the pueblo. He took with his three sons, who ranged in age from eighteen to seven.

When they reached the petrol station they found the old man hammering away at the concrete with his chisel. "You won't find no oil down there, hombre," said the butcher with a smirk. His sons stood behind him nervously. "Even if you do, it's not your property so not your petrol," he continued.

The old man stopped his hammering and met the man's gaze. All around him were small piles of broken up concrete and sandy soil. "Oil?" he asked distractedly. "I seek not death but life." Alfonso and his sons looked at the old man with his long grey beard and his worn and tattered clothing. The butcher repeated what he had just said about it being someone else's property and warned the old man not to go digging up stuff that didn't belong to him. Then they turned and left, setting off back along the road in the direction of the pueblo at a brisk pace, stout walking sticks in hand. The youngest son trailed behind the others, casting a backward glance as he went. The old man caught him with his eye and the boy swiftly turned away, as if he was afraid the old man might harm him. When they were mere dots on the horizon of the north road the old man got back to work. "Perhaps," he muttered to himself. "Perhaps."

On the fourth day the hole was big enough for the old man to stand in with his head just level with the ground. Mud oozed between his toes and he closed his eyes, giving thanks. The Fifth Garden could now begin, and for this he cried tears of happiness. As he slept that night he felt as though he left his body. He turned and looked at the ragged old man lying beneath the stars on the rickshaw and what he saw made him laugh. From the hole in the concrete on the forecourt there came all manner of life. There were water elementals, as well as those of fire and air, and there were earth spirits—the *duende* of old—released after being imprisoned for so long, as well as the spirits of trees, called *dryads* by some, and plants and animals and the ghosts of long deceased people. They all danced joyously, at first around the hole but then around the whole land and even the sky above, and when the old man awoke with the morning sun he felt half exhausted. He chuckled to himself as he unfolded his tired limbs from the rickshaw, planting his bare feet on the dusty concrete for another day's work.

From the rickshaw he took an old plastic sack and slung it over one shoulder. The day was spent poking around in ditches with a long, hooked stick, pulling out plastic bottles and faded red and orange aluminium cans still bearing the inscriptions of old. When he had filled the sack he returned to the petrol station and poured them out on the ground with a tremendous clatter. Taking a knife from a pouch on his belt he sat down and began to fashion the bottles and aluminium cans into open-topped containers, which he set up in rows. When this was completed he returned to the ditch with a small spade and began to dig. Most of the soil was dry and dusty but the old man knew it would be better than the arid sun-parched earth lying on the surface. He put the soil into bags, carefully sifting out the ring pulls, cigarette butts and plastic debris with his fingers. He then carried the filtered soil over to the petrol station and filled each container with love and care, gently tamping down the soil and placing a single seed into each container. For each seed he took from the collection he had amassed from the Fourth Garden, he said a short prayer for its successful germination.

But there was a stage he had forgotten. He scouted around and came back with four good-sized flat rocks and a short length of metal pipe, which he threw down into the hole and then climbed down himself. From these he fashioned a platform on which to place a vessel, and a font from which the water would trickle. It wasn't much more than a trickle, but that would be good enough, he mused.

An old paint tin with a wire handle was attached to a piece of nylon rope and dropped into the hole where it filled with the trickling water. The old man tasted it. It was as sweet and fresh as anything he had tasted in the Third Garden, which had been high up in the snow capped mountains of the south. From the tin he watered the seeds and by the end of the first day 240 plastic and aluminium containers housed the sleeping seeds of the Fifth Garden.

Near the old petrol station stood an ancient olive tree. It had stood on that spot since before the birth of Christ and, as such, thought it had seen it all. Its bark was scaly and its growth stunted from years of drought, but its roots were long and deep and it had managed to persist while all around it had perished. The old man went and sat with his back against it for a while and rested. "If you give me a spell I will give you my body in return," he eventually said to the tree. The tree seemed to think about this for a great long time. It was not impressed by humans or the things they got up to, and it wasn't particularly in the mood for helping this one out. Nevertheless, just as the sun was going down, the tree made up its woody mind and a deal was struck between the two.

After the day had ended and the land was aching out its heat a cataract of cloud slid in front of the stars. It brought with it a rainless night of silent forked lightning that lit up the cantankerous old olive tree in monochrome flashes. The old man tossed and turned and moved in and out of a dreamless sleep. That night there was no dancing with *dryads* and *duendes*, and the sound of the wild dogs seemed to get closer. A single clap of thunder sounded in the deepest part of the night, causing everybody for miles around to sit up in bed and cross themselves. It was as loud as an atomic bomb, and it sent people scurrying under the bedclothes in fear. By morning the clouds had dispersed and another hot and rainless day awaited the old man and the people in the pueblo.

The local children had been scared by the storm and the youngest of the butcher's sons—who went by the name of Alfonsito - told his friends the old man had likely caused it. "That old wizard's digging for petrol and using it to make spells," he said to his wide-eyed friends. "If we kill him we'll save everyone in the pueblo," he said, puffing up his chest.

A few days later, when they had plucked up the courage to do so, little Alfonsito took two friends on a mission to go and kill the old man. They rode out on bicycles that had been lovingly crafted by their parents with solid rubber tyres, wooden brake blocks and chains lubricated with olive oil. When they got close to the old petrol station they hid the bikes in scrub by the roadside and went forwards on foot. Alfonsito carried a catapult and had a bag of stones at the ready, and his friends were armed with sticks sharpened to points. "I will knock him out with a stone and then you will push the stakes through his heart," he said. "Okay," they replied, quivering in fear.

But when they got to the petrol station the old man was nowhere to be found. After a period of observation to make sure of this the boys rushed onto the forecourt and in one hot minute caused as much damage as they could. They pushed over the rickshaw and kicked over the seeds in their containers, spilling soil all over the concrete. A small stove with a kettle and pan was kicked into the hole and Alfonsito—excitement and fear having got the better of him—unleashed a squirt of yellow urine onto some bedding in a hammock that hung between two fuel pumps. And then, squealing like wild piglets, they ran off back into the desert to their bikes.

When the old man returned from his bottle-collecting foray he surveyed the scene of devastation. Expressionless, he set down the sack of containers and began to clear up the mess. As he carefully repotted the seeds in their containers a smile played across his lips and he raised his eyes to the old olive tree. *Perhaps*, he thought.

In the pueblo, word got out about what the boys had done. Despite swearing themselves to secrecy one of them had boasted about the episode at Sunday school and soon everyone knew about it. Their parents were furious, but none more so than Alfonsito's. His father was known for being cruel to the goats and sheep people brought him to be butchered, and it was rumoured that his cruelty extended to his own family. Each boy received a beating with a leather belt that night. "Don't go messing with strangers," they said. "Getting tangled up with outsiders will only lead to trouble in this day and age," they warned.

As the weeks and months went by the people from the pueblo began to accept the presence of the old man, whom they nicknamed Petroleo. Why he would want to live in the old Shell station nobody could fathom. Only the surviving old could remember what the petrol station had been like back in the day, when everything was shiny and refrigerated and the cars sped along on the smooth tarmac road. Back then they'd thought it would go on like that forever. The petrol station had been a place to hang out and rev your engine as you watched the *chicas* pull up on their scooters to buy cigarettes and flash their eyes at the boys. There was music there sometimes, and you could buy chilled beer from a cabinet inside. But the cars and the scooters were all long gone now, mostly broken up and taken away by scrap merchants, although there were a few at the bottom of the steep-sided gully outside the pueblo. Several more still littered the desert too, called "poor men's tombs" and left well alone.

A chill wind had arisen in the south, just as it did every year with the onset of cooler weather, and the clouds that gathered over the distant sierra appeared like the UFOs of ancient folklore. The old man set to work with his mattock. He knew the rains would soon be upon them and eagerly anticipated their arrival. *So much work to do*, he muttered as he set off to survey the land around him and devise a plan. The rains would come in like a wild beast, that much he knew. They would lash the dry earth, turning the dusty surface into torrents of sticky grey and yellow mud. The window of time in which the plants and the seeds could make use of this annual gift would be narrow, and the old man knew his job was to open it wider. He lifted the mattock over his head and behind his back and brought it down again in an arc. The dry land threw up dust and loose stones with each blow, but by the end of the day the first section of earth bank was dug. After a week it would resemble a long and sinuous snake lying on the land at the foot of a knoll, with a trench on its inner side nestled against the lower slope. The old man looked at his work with satisfaction, and then raised his eyes to take in the landscape that spread around him. The thought of the work he still had to do did not faze him. *Patience*, he said to himself. *Anything is achievable with patience.* This was, after all, his *Fifth* Garden.

The first drop of rain came in late November. The old man kept track of time by watching the natural world around him. When the bee-eaters left it meant summer was over. Then when the cicadas stopped it would only be three weeks before the first rains. The positions of the rising and the setting sun and moon were worth noting too, but he also followed the dates in an almanac he kept in a leather saddlebag in the rickshaw. It was here he kept forty years of notes written in a small cramped hand that now filled two dozen notebooks. Everything was in there. The types of seed he had harvested, the planting times relative to the lunar phases, the elevation and aspect of the sites, the species of insect encountered, which plant guilds worked best together, the dreams he had had about the plants—all in summary form along with all the successes and the failures of a life of practice. If doing was the old man's yin, then learning was his yang, and he reminded himself of this every day. *I am just a child, playing in the sand,* he would sing to himself.

When the rains finally broke, great dark curtains swept across the land and blotted out the sky. The old man sheltered under the roof of the petrol station and moved the seedlings in their bottles out into the open. Water raged in torrents down gullies, flooding certain areas and scouring hills down to bedrock in others. For days he ran around with his mattock, making repairs to his earthworks, adjusting the flow of the streams and noting the way the water behaved in relation to the contours of the land. In quiet moments between downpours the air was filled with the sound of chirruping frogs in the old ditch where the old man had first heard one call out to him that night half a year ago. The ditch was now freshly dug out and dammed at each end and it had filled with clear water. Lush green shoots poked through the surface of the water and in the spring there would be dragonflies and swallows and hummingbirds. *Well I never*, mused the old man.

The people in the pueblo, for the most part, continued to ignore the old man and his digging, thinking old Petroleo was likely mad but harmless. In any case, they reasoned, there were plenty of folk around who were mad but *not* harmless.

Nevertheless, children were warned not to go near him, for one could never be too sure in these times. A local shepherd had offered him a goat and he had taken it with thanks but did not slaughter it. Instead it followed him around as he worked and the old man sang to it and took it on long walks in the desert. Rumour grew that he didn't eat anything, and seemed to live off fresh air and moonbeams.

When the rains had died down to the occasional shower the old man set about planting the land with grasses. One passer-by from the pueblo had seen him crawling around the desert on his hands and knees, and developed the opinion that he was talking to the ants. Rather, he was diligently poking tiny seeds into holes in the ground, taking care not to waste a single one from his limited supply. As ever, he said a short prayer as each seed went into the ground. They were of different varieties. A smoke bush here, a broom there, grasses and hardy succulents—the old man had a pattern in his head that he hoped to manifest into reality, just as he had done in the other gardens. He was confident in all that he did.

By April the rains had eased off and the early results of his work were beginning to show. Everywhere within a one-minute walk's radius around the old petrol station was beginning to come to life. Tiny seedlings broke out from the sterile subsoils of the desert and it wasn't long before the ground took on a green sheen. The old man jumped for joy and rushed around the land during every moment of daylight with his watering can. The plants in the bottles began to awaken too. There were oranges, lemons, almonds, pomegranates, oaks, olives and a hundred others all putting up slender stems and unfurling tender green leaves. He tied the young goat to the gnarled olive tree and warned it not to go near the Garden. "There's plenty of herbs and bushes for you to eat over yonder," he said, gesturing to the hills. "You keep your beady eyes off my little children."

As the days lengthened and warmed the old man's pace became more frenetic. He knew every plant in the garden; knew how much water it needed and when, and knew if it was feeling sick or unwell. He had, in the back of the rickshaw, a large glass bottle filled with a viscous black liquid. Every now and then he would pour a few drops of it into a bottle of spring water and make a tonic for the revival of any of the young plants that seemed to be flagging. It didn't always work and in the first year around a third of the plants were lost. "Such is life," said the old man cheerily as he planted up the next year's seeds.

In the second year of the Fifth Garden the old man expanded to a two minutes' radius walk from the old Shell garage. The goat had grown big from eating the spiny bushes in the hills, and the old man walked it on a lead and allowed it to nibble down the grasses he had planted the previous year. As it munched it dropped its dung on the ground and the old man dug it in around the stems of the young plants with his bony fingers. There were pools and ditches full of water wherever one looked and the land was starting to hum with insects and butterflies. This brought him joy but when the winter came he felt age creeping into his bones and prayed for just a few more years so that his work could be finished. On starlit summer nights he still danced with the *duende* and the *dryads*, always returning to his old body just before sunrise for another day of planting and watering and digging and tending.

The seasons rolled by and, year-by-year, the Fifth Garden expanded outwards from the old petrol station like a slowly growing green stain in the yellow desert. One goat became three, and a donkey arrived too, simply turning up one day in a state of emaciation and thirst. The old man nursed it back to health and it too became a part of the Fifth Garden. Chickens roamed and pecked at insects and the old man collected their eggs and gave them as gifts to passers by on the old north road. "What's in it for you?" they would ask, suspiciously, and the old man would laugh and tell them they were gifts from his heart. "All I ask," he would tell them "is that I show you my garden."

In this way he would lead them gently by the arm and take them around the land, pointing at young trees and shrubs and plucking fruit as they went. Inevitably, by the time the stranger left the garden, their arms would be full of pomegranates and melons and the small orange fruits that were called *nisperos*. The old man, his back now hunched from years of planting and tending the land, would totter over to the hammock and lie down. "Not long now," he would mutter. "Not long." Sometimes a pair of eyes spied on him, watching and waiting.

In the ninth year of the Fifth Garden the old man was all but spent. Each morning when his soul returned from dancing with the *duende* and the *dryads* it found a body not unlike a sack of dry sticks from the old riverbed, wizened and contorted by pain. Cataracts clouded his eyes and it became ever harder for him to walk the goats and the donkey, to water the plants with the tin can on a rope and to carry firewood back to his little kettle and stove. Beyond the garden, in the yellow dust of the desert with its cracked and broken trees and its bare rocks, the figure still lurked. It watched the old man from afar, unsure and sad and torn between two worlds.

"Time's up," said the old man under his breath one morning. He was scrutinising his almanac as a handful of twigs on a fire heated up the copper kettle. It was ten years to the day since the frog had called out to him. He waited for the kettle to boil and poured the water into a cup into which a mixture of dry herbs and berries had been placed. He then drank the bitter drink slowly. Was he being watched today? He felt that he was. He closed his eyes and said a prayer. For an hour he sat still without moving, as if in a deep trance. When he opened his eyes again a tear rolled down his wizened cheeks. It was time.

He arose unsteadily and walked into the garden. All that his old eyes could discern was a green blur stretching around him. The soft morning sun warmed his face and dried his tears and he walked over to his animals and, one by one, stroked their heads and murmured his goodbyes. When he was done he began to walk up the path in the direction of the gnarled old olive. "I have come to give you my side of the bargain," he called out. But something stopped him in his tracks. For although his eyesight was nearly gone his sense of hearing was as keen as the day he was born and what he heard made him fall to his knees. He crawled towards the sound, brushing aside huge soft leaves and vines as he tried to locate the source. And there it was. He leaned closer to look, his face almost touching the sweet water as it flowed from the ground and trickled over the rocks. He leaned in closer. "Is that you?" he cried excitedly. "Is it you?"

Later, when Alfonsito found him, the old man was curled up in a foetal position like a baby. A single dark brown frog sat on a rock a few inches from the old man's face as if it were guarding his body, hopping away into the stream when the teenager bent down. "I'm sorry," Alfonsito cried out. "I didn't mean to do it. My father told me you were evil and I believed him. But he beat me and tormented me over the years and all I wanted to do was come and learn from you and to escape. And now it's too late." The teenager bent forward and sobbed, but there was nobody to hear his anguish, just the gentle chatter of the stream pouring forth from between two rocks and the buzz of the cicadas in the cherry trees. At length he picked up the old man's body in his arms and took it to the gnarled old olive. The grave had already been dug by the old man.

That night Alfonsito slept beside the tree under the canopy of the stars. In his dreams he left his body and danced around the land and in the sky with the *duende* and the *dryads* and he had never known such happiness and joy. Among them there danced a sprightly figure with twinkling eyes and a bushy black beard. "Here, take my hand," he said to Alfonsito.

When he awoke the sun was creeping up over the eastern sierra. Alfonsito packed everything into the rickshaw and untied the animals, hitching the donkey between the pulling bars. The young man walked away from the petrol station, setting out on the cracked and potholed north road. After a few minutes he stopped and turned for one last look at the only place he had ever known. The pueblo lay in the dun-coloured landscape, low and dusty and faded. There was nothing remarkable about the place; it was just like any other, except that in the foreground there spread a green oasis. Already the Fifth Garden was beginning to lose its circular shape, and tendrils of green had started to snake out from it, exploring their way across the landscape. The young man turned and departed. As the land began to soak up the heat from the sun above, so too began his quest to seek out the First Garden.

Revival

by Ian O'Reilly

They came by ones and twos out of the eaves of New Wood. The cindered light of the winter sun was starting to fade behind them, casting cold faces and chapped lips in reds and pinks. A few murmured greetings, solemn, reserved; everyone instinctively knew that now was not a time for the niceties of neighbours.

Ali paused on the path, letting the others carry on towards the hollow in the headland beyond. All around their spit of land swelled the choppy Atlantic sea. His teeth chattered. His hands, thrust into their woollen mittens inside his homespun jacket, still ached with the approaching cold. The wind off the coast was always bitter, but in the middle of winter it had teeth. The young man knew that they'd be lucky if they didn't have a frost in the morning. He stamped his cold feet once again.

But I wouldn't trade this for a warm house nor bed, he thought, looking to where the reflected reds of the sunset burned a broken path on the wave tops far below, growing ever fainter the further out the light reached into the night, like the endless days fading into history behind them.

Ali shook out his long fringe, wishing that he hadn't shaved one side of his head this last autumn gone. *How long have people being coming up here, on this night? Waiting up, watching the last rays of the sun stretch like that?* He didn't know the answer to that. It had only been a couple of years that he had been allowed to come up here on his own. *Old enough to fall into the sea on your own!* He smiled, recalling the Alderman's rough words. Not that it happened, at least, not in Ali's lifetime. People knew to keep in the circle of the firelight that was about to be born—

WHOOSH!

The bonfires around the circular hollow were contained in five rust-covered metal bins, filled with carefully layered stacks of sweet and hot woods like cherry and rowan. Each bin had holes punched through its body, so that they would cast hot shards of light over the celebration like miniature suns. The piles of wood had already been doused in some of the Lighters' precious oil, and as they burst into life the smell of something caustic and greasy wafted over the gathering horde for a second, but was quickly replaced by the sweeter smell of the woods. Later on in the night, Ali knew, the anonymous figures known as Lighters with their fantastical masks of beasts and lurid faces would replace these "hot" woods with longer-burning oaks and yew.

Every fire-containing bin was wider than Ali could stretch his arms from fingertip to fingertip. He'd asked what they had been, once, before they became fire-holders, and the Lighters had just shaken their head, wordlessly. Whatever these cylindrical segments had once been, their use now was to keep the people warm through the longest night, and ward off the darkness.

Ali felt his steps unconsciously quicken as the last fire was lit. He was heading down towards the hollow, where the only other structures were the scattered remains of the old cement blocks that littered the world now—clearly the foundations of some building from ages past, and now huddled like grandfathers on market day.

Is it now? Is it now? he found himself thinking, craning his head to peer over the excited, breathless faces of the others at the last glimmers of ruddy sunset-light.

Almost. This is it . . . Ali held his breath, watching as with a final flash—

The sun was gone.

The young man loved this moment. It was as if the whole world paused, just for the briefest of heartbeats, wondering whether to carry on with the business of night time and winters and stars and, hopefully, eventual dawns.

"H'YARRGH!" With an animal convulsion the crowd around him roared, and Ali found himself joining in the shouting and yelling. People cheered the last year, they growled at the long night ahead, they whooped with joy and defiance. In that moment, the silence broke and the drums began.

The drummers were from every walk of life, young and old. People brought their own rough hand-held drums, or wood-bound casks that were beaten with felt-tipped mallets. Still more tapped and played with palms and fingers and the heels of hands, rising like a crescendo, finding a rhythm; a pattern; a pulse.

The cheering, still-shouting crowd rushed into the space between the concrete slabs, lit not by sunset this time but by the orange and yellow glow of the fire-cylinders.

And they started to dance.

‡‡

Eyes glinting or half closed in reverie; teeth—flashing, bared. Feet stamped on the earth bare or in moccasin boots. Legs braced, stretched, thighs strained with constant movement. Hips swayed, rocked, swung, torsos spun, twirled, and arms flung outwards as the people of the coast moved.

Ali didn't know how long he danced, or even with how many people. It was a mess of laughter, drum-roar, and bodies between the circle of flames.

The revellers crushed and pressed near the centre of the hollow, but by some natural eddy a constant current of people kept renewing and retiring from the vortex. Ali circled around the centre space three, four, six times; first, dancing with this Chinese woman, then with a laughing young man with fair hair. He forgot how many times he had stamped and swayed around the circle. It was as endless as the days that whirled behind them, back to the past, or as the sun that hurled itself over the world day after day, year after year, age after age.

There were people that he recognised from the village: the couple who ran the bakery, the gaggle of youngsters who worked in the field. Some of the wildest dancers were the ones who lifted each other up, spinning into the air above the crowd of assorted scouts, explorers and expeditioners who travelled far and wide across this dark continent, carrying news from one settlement to another, bearing tidings, and searching the decaying cities for anything left of value.

Quietly, Ali bid them all the joy they might find; their role was one of the harshest ones, besides the sea-fishers and the hunters, and not many came back each autumn.

But what sights they must see! the young man thought, *remembering the stories of dams that held back entire lakes, bridges that spanned islands, and lands which were nothing but hot sand and metal towers—*

Ali's thoughts whirled away from him, just as his feet did in their own primal axis.

Some of the people there wore masks, others wore their best finery. Veils, cloaks, wraps and sarongs dyed with the brightest of madder, indigo, or the rare chemical dyes you might find in a sunken supermarket. Others wore feathers hunted from the eagles and kingfishers found around here, or bracelets made of ring-pulls and shells. The people danced for themselves or each other, but they all danced.

Ali laughed, the joy bubbling up through him as undeniable as the gravity underfoot. Hands were on his shoulders, and he was looking into the eyes of a girl with dark skin who laughed as she pressed a flask of something into his hands. It tasted sharp like wine, but also fragrant like elderflowers. Still laughing, Ali pushed the flask into the hands of the next reveller, the drink reminding him just how tired he was. He stumbled out of the circle—

‡‡

—to collapse near one of the metal bins, his back up against one of the concrete slabs that reared its geometry precisely, tens of feet above him. It felt steadying for his spinning head. He was tired—*No, I am exhausted*, he corrected himself—but still, amazingly, the others carried on the dance behind him, just as they would carry on towards dawn.

But for me? Ali groaned happily, rubbing some life back into his legs as he caught his breath, looking out into the dark beyond the firelight.

It was hard to see into the darkness with the fire so close, but by shielding his hand he could make out a deeper line of murk that must be the coast, a *slightly greyer* that must be the sea.

A few stars out tonight, he noted, allowing the strange feeling of the empty world before him to float upwards. He wondered just how far that darkness spread. Did it encircle the whole globe?

Was this the only fire to be seen, if you could look down from on high—far, far up there?

As if in answer to his unspoken question, one of the Lighters came to crouch down a few feet away, looking out into the darkness. This Lighter had long red curls sprouting from a mask like a bird's beak. Idly, the slightly intoxicated Ali wondered if he knew her in real life.

"Hell of a sight," the Lighter murmured, nodding towards the grey and tiny silver flickers of wavetops that stretched in all directions across the cold Atlantic. "Seems like it should go on forever, don't it?"

Ali knew what the Lighter was doing. She was making small talk: companionable, agreeable nothings to make sure that Ali was still able to talk, and not so drunk that he was about to collapse or wander off into the woods or sea on his own.

Not that there aren't plenty of drunk people wandering off into the woods tonight, he thought, *but that is a different matter altogether—*

"Anyone ever got to the other side?" Ali found himself asking, before feeling immediately stupid. *Of course they had. They used to, didn't they? They used to travel all the time across the sea . . .*

"I mean, today . . ." he added lamely, realizing that he probably *was* drunker than he had thought.

The Lighter chuckled. "I know what you mean, and no." She shook her head. "Although, you know Arla? The scout from Three-Rivers? She says that she found a community right the way up to the north who said they were building a boat that could do it. Twin-hulled yacht that they're going to take to Greenland, and from there to Iceland, and then down into Europe."

"No shit, really?" Ali pushed himself up against the concrete block, trying to find a word for the silver-flecked sea in front of them, and the *vastness* of the undertaking. "That's . . . that's *big*."

Idiot, he thought to himself.

"Yeah. You should ask her about it if you're interested, if you can get her to stop throwing Jess around. She told me that it's been done before, many times, and these guys she met have probably as much chance as anyone else . . ." The Lighter pointed with her mask-beak back to where the dancing was the most exuberant. "You never know, maybe she'll take you with her on her next trip? You can see for yourself?"

"Yeah, maybe." Ali shook his head. He still had *no* idea what he was going to do. At the moment he worked at pretty much everything and anything around the village: laboured in the field, helped with the lambing when spring came, chopped wood, stacked wood, carded fleece. . . . What would he do out there, as a scout?

But still . . . just imagine that? All the way across the oceans . . .

"Maybe." Again, Ali had that feeling of the vastness of the night and the sea around them, and that they were just a small bubble of floating warmth and cheer in an endless night. It was comforting to be here, to feel the pulse and pound of feet on the frosted earth, of drums echoing against the concrete megaliths.

But it wasn't endless, was it? Ali's alcohol-soaked mind thought back to the lessons he'd had in the village. Of the Alderman trying to lecture them out of crumbling books, shouting at them not to touch the fragile paper, pointing to the maps of a world that they had inherited—

"There's others out there," Ali was saying, "on the other side of the ocean."

"That's what we think," the Lighter agreed. "What do *you* think?"

Ali thought about the sea and the faded maps, the pulse of the drums and the warm press of bodies behind him. "I think that there is probably a hundred, a hundred-hundred fires out there in the dark tonight, on the longest night of winter." He could feel the *rightness* of his words even as he said them. *I mean, what else do you do at the darkest point? The point furthest from the dawn? You build a light. You keep the fire burning. You go on.*

With a laughing groan, the older Lighter stood up from her crouch, protesting about her knees. "Well I think you're right too. Come on, up you get before you get too cold." Ali accepted her hand and pulled himself up to his feet, still a little unsteady, but sober enough to dance.

"Go on, there's a way to go before dawn yet, but I think you'll make it." The Lighter nodded, pushing him gently, back into the circle of warmth, light, and smiling faces.

CASCADE

BY CATHERINE McGUIRE

Rya threw down the wet tunic. "Crap! Broke another nail! Marel's tunics have too many buttons!"

She sucked on her sore finger and stared across the river, ignoring the pounding of rock on fabric, the chatting women on the bank and the laughing of distant guards. The usual rage welled up, but she stuffed it back down. Across the brown water, beyond the town on the far bank, the sun rose over Bleak Peak. She turned—Cascade Falls's towers rose above the timbered ringwall protecting its thatched homes. Their salvaged bricks were now gilded to a bronzy red-gold, and under crenellations where large crossbows glinted, two ancient-color panels were displayed. Rya drank in the glowing pinks, turquoise, and colors for which there were no names. All salvage, including old-color, was distributed among the five towns ringing the ancient city, but raids to capture treasured old-color objects, brighter than anything now possible, necessitated the crossbows. So the elders said—there hadn't been any local skirmishes during Rya's lifetime. Unless one counted the squabbling among burghers and town councilmun.

Even at midsummer, the river damp seeped through Rya's linen tunic, and splashed water was chilling. Again she kicked herself for signing into debt service. And with Marel Quiller, the world's surliest woman! Well, the world as far as Bleak Peak, anyway, as far as anyone had traveled.

"Woolgathering again? You're credited by hours *worked*, not wasted." Tyra's tone was light, but Rya knew she'd tattle to Marel as soon as they got back to the house. Rya bent to the washing.

Once laundry had been pounded and rinsed, it had to be lugged back—dripping, twice as heavy—up the stone-lined path and through the river gate, where bored guards harassed any woman not rich enough for her own bodyguard. The half-dozen women from various grand homes laundered as a group each Wednesday to protect each other.

"Good morning my little brown nut! That lovely black hair would look stunning draped on my chest." The tallest guard sounded like he'd had some education; unfortunately the others had been educated in the stables.

"It would look better draped lower down," one hooted. The tall one frowned—Rya suspected he liked her, but she never gave him time to follow up. She sped through the gates with the others.

Cascade Falls was waking up, the streets filling with tradesmen and early guard patrol. Shutters were taken down and goods hung by shop doors. Even after two years, Rya found things worth looking at and she slowed her pace. The town had grown during its hundred years—storytellers said some fields had once been within the timber walls, but now it was crammed to the edge with thatched one- and two-story shop-homes, a stable for twenty-five horses, an adjoining blacksmith, a school now cramped with fifty students, a glazier, a prison near the river gate, two large water cisterns laboriously filled from the river in summer, the Goddess Tower catty-corner from the Council building in the central square, which was in fact a couple blocks from the town center. It was typical of Cascade Falls that no one was allowed to mention that. Most structures were mud stucco over wattle, some with pastel milk-paint, but official buildings were salvaged stone and brick, and their shallow-carved images and colored tile were mysterious remnants of what had been. Four official old-color sculptures—twisted metal welded in puzzling shapes—drew appreciative crowds: reds and blues surpassing the loveliest flowers, golds and purples like the richest sunsets. Each stood out from the mud-brown streets like a wild poppy in a dying field. Some wealthy merchants had their own displays—dangling bits of transparent color like ice that wasn't cold, flashing in the sun under their protective eye.

Definitely, Cascade Falls was one of the more sophisticated towns ringing old Port Lann. There was even a library with writings from the lost civilizations, but Rya had never been inside. Her contract was read to her before she signed, and the only writing she understood was on safety posters. Rya noticed one as they turned off Main: "Danger! Hot oil." That was the energy plant, which recycled fats and cooking oil, occasionally splashing out on unwary passersby. It didn't stink as bad as the night-soil gasmaker's, but bad enough. The night-soil carts had already made the rounds; they were mandated off the streets an hour after dawn.

"See you next week!" The washer women waved as they turned off to their employers' homes. Rya and Tyra crossed town to the Hill Gate section, where houses had their own courtyards and outbuildings.

‡‡

The sun was well up before they got the wash hung on ropes strung between the garden hut and the foodstore. Rya envied the bright-hued sheets, tunics, trousers, tablecloths. Marel was rich enough to afford dyes *and* embroidery, and vain enough to indulge herself. She had some old-color trinkets as sun-catchers in front of her bedroom window: long bent icicles of almost indescribable color, mysterious and fragile, probably costing as much as all her fine garments combined. But she could afford it. As a widow, she was unhindered by a partner's needs, and she certainly gave no thought to her debt servants! Rya's stomach already rumbled with hunger, having worked off the pre-dawn meal and then some. She stowed the wicker clothes basket and hurried to the garden, to help hoe and maybe palm a couple green beans. Today was FreeFest, so she'd be needed soon to help Marel dress and primp. The thought of the ceremony of release, where debt servants signed their completed contracts, roiled inside. Rya should have been free this year, but Marel was devious, and somehow Rya could never catch up. Theoretically, debt service traded six days' and evenings' work for room, board and enough additional payment that the debtor was released with money and/or the skills to start life anew. But incomplete or avoided work incurred penalties—and somehow Rya could never get it right.

Dew still clung to the leaves, ephemeral diamonds glinting in sunlight. The daily miracle, life abounding, always lifted her spirits. Even after ancient catastrophes had done much harm to the land, there was enough and they were rediscovering edible plants every year. Food, like salvage, was theoretically shared among all, but one look at the hefty burghers and their scrawny servants revealed the lie. This town decreed that food be divided by portion, rather than giving more to those who worked harder physically. As a result, those who sat around waving their hands to be obeyed grew plump. And of course they were the only ones who could decide to change the decree.

At least today she'd be able to meet Danel, share a salted prezzel and a cozy chat in some out-of-the-way place. Marel would be paraded in her sedan chair, preening with the wealthy as they showed their power and supposed generosity. Bile rose in her throat at the thought. Cascade Falls had a reputation as resource-full and secure, which was why she'd chosen it after she'd sold her mother's loom to pay for Kira's dowry. Before that, she and her little sister had been doing fine, not rich but not hungry, in the village of River Stones. Without the tools of her trade, Rya had chosen debt service for two years, or so she'd thought. Cascade Falls' wealth was in the hands of a few, who bent the laws of Township like prezzels to keep it.

"Rya! You're needed by the lady," Obun hollered from the back door.

"How much does she pay you for calling her a lady?" Rya joked.

"All the gold I can eat," he retorted with a saucy smile.

Obun was a scruffy redhead far smaller than his supposed fifteen years. Rya suspected he was about eleven, making his debt service illegal. Counselors, influenced by Marel's kegs of ale, had ignored Rya's cautious complaint, decreeing there was no birth certificate, therefore no proof.

"Well, see if you can sneak into town today to eat something more nourishing," she called out as she passed.

The stucco-and-beam house was impressive—two floors with five rooms each. It had a grand front stairs and a narrow service backstairs. Though not as massive as councilors' mansions, it was twice the size of its neighbors. She tiptoed up the backstairs and eased toward the front bedroom, grateful for the green-gold braided carpet muffling her steps. She heard chatting—it always paid to find out what people were saying behind her back. Not that she traded in gossip, like many—this was purely self defense. Marel encouraged backstabbing and drama so none of the debt servants had any leftover energy.

"Berl still has a fine head of hair, and his lands outside the Pale stretch all along Dry Creek."

That was Marel's hairdresser. So they were still discussing marriage prospects. Rya didn't believe Marel would marry again—why give up her freedom, even if technically partners were equal? Marel preferred being dictator. And it was common knowledge Marel used her stablehand for pleasure, despite the risk of him accusing her of sexual coercion.

"Berl bulges like a full wine sack," Marel complained. Her voice was thin and raspy, as if she couldn't be bothered to push the words out. "Tomson is sleek and well-hung."

And twenty years younger, Rya thought. He was her age, son of the mayor, and not likely to be angling for the hand of a matron who fitted into her clothes like a stuffed sausage.

"Where *is* that slack-off?" Marel fretted. Rya hurried through the door and grabbed the heavy corset on the bed. "It's about time! When I call, you make it your *priority*."

"Yes ma'am." Rya didn't bother to look apologetic. She took the corset from Tyra and held it until the hairdresser had tucked the last gray-flecked auburn braid into the gold net, and pinned everything to the bronze circlet on Marel's head. Of course getting her hair done first made dressing *much* more complicated—Marel knew that well.

There was no chatting as they strapped Marel into the heavy, boned contraption—it was tricky finding the balance between a pleasing shape and being able to breathe. Fortunately Marel did this only twice a year, when she wore her floor length gown. Mostly she dressed in tunics and pants, rich but normal clothing. But today's competition would be fierce—the ladies of town draped with their wealth, painted pack mules acting like Pharohes. Rya was hazy on what those had been, since school only lasted four years before apprenticeship, but she knew they'd been associated with gold sometime in the misty past. They'd lived in triangular mansions and flew on big metal birds. Something like that. There were no such buildings nearby, but salvage had reduced the city near Cascade Falls to shoulder-high rubble and unusable fragments.

Finally the fit was approved and Rya reached for the white undergown with scarlet embroidered sleeves. She dropped it carefully over Marel's waiting arms.

"Gently! You're too fast! Are you as impatient with your lovers?" Marel's voice was muffled but clear enough that the hairdresser and Tyra, dusting Marel's clutter of antiques, snickered. Rya bit back a reply. Marel insisted on Rya's attendance to exact her pound of flesh, not because Rya had skill. Rya adjusted the shift and turned to get the heavy indigo wool gown subtly woven with scarlet threads.

"Tongue too tired to talk?" Marel sneered. "You must have been using it hard last night."

"Don't measure everyone with your own tape," Rya snapped before she could stop herself. Oh well—in for a penny . . . "I'm sure your *mount* is well *groomed* for today."

Marel hissed but had no comeback—maybe she remembered Rya besting her last time. Marel was crude but dull-witted; Rya's remarks could tear the flesh off someone. And there were witnesses. Rya gestured at the hairdresser to help lower the gown over the coif and they managed with only one strand knocked loose, but of course that was what Marel complained about. Rya ignored her and went to the jewel box.

"I want the Starfish lady," Marel snapped.

Rya lifted the necklace by its multicolored glass beads. The metal pendant was a thin embossed green-and-white oval cut from ancient salvage; a lady with a double fishtail, wearing a crown. Legend said she was the Goddess of Sleep and Wakefulness. Her images were salvaged everywhere, especially little bags of shiny unwoven cloth so fragile they only survived in display cases.

Once Marel was arrayed as she wished, with earrings of pounded silver and polished turquoise and a bracelet of antique buttons etched with glittering insects, she dismissed Rya to assist with lunch. "And don't eat first! Or cook too much."

"I know Madame eats like a bird," Rya replied. "I've seen vultures feast," she added in a lower voice that was still audible.

"I'll have you before the burghers for insolence!" Marel's rage followed her down the hall.

She couldn't risk more time owed—she was down to two meals a day so she wouldn't owe for three, and yesterday she'd elbowed the maid aside before she could smash a vase and blame Rya. On Marel's order, she was sure. There *had* to be a way out! She needed someone to read her contract again—Marel kept quoting new rules. Rya didn't trust the Council; she needed an honest outsider! She had some hand-woven linen, a precious keepsake, but maybe as payment?

Midday meal was potatoes cooked with kale and a little butter. Instead of chicken broth they were boiled in water, so it was bland, but filling. She suspected Marel's portion was spiced, but the cook was sly and there'd be no unfairness to report. The five house servants ate together at the kitchen table, chatting about today's ceremony. Michel the yard man was being released.

"Let us in on your secret," the cook teased. "We all want to get out."

"Did you have to give special services like the stablehand?" the maid asked.

Michel laughed. "No, though I could have. My service was more *diplomatic*." He refused to elaborate.

Probably covering up for something, Rya mused. Did he realize that put him in her power even after release? He didn't look bright.

The cook came down after delivering Marel's meal, and reported that she'd ordered Rya to stay behind and watch the place, and clean the pantry shelves and floor.

"I won't bother you with her insults," the cook told Rya. "I'm sure you can imagine."

"Oh, yes," Rya said sourly. She watched as the others hurried out to join the stablehand and gardener waiting with the sedan chair out front.

Ten minutes later, Rya was scrubbing the pantry shelves, fuming. This was makework! On the other hand, she wasn't having to dance attendance on Marel. And it was quiet. And scrubbing worked off some of her anger. She removed the jars, jugs and boxes from the top shelf and, using a keg as stool, reached all the way back to get the cobwebs and dust. Marel wasn't going to find *anything* wrong with *this* job!

As she swirled the rag into the corner, it caught something more solid than web—an old label? It was too dark to see, so Rya fished with the rag until it was graspable. She pulled it forward—a small roll of parchment tied with string, stained and slightly torn. Impulsively, Rya unfolded it—some kind of writing. It looked official, with large writing on top and lots of bunched words in the center, and then two signatures. What was it doing there??

A thump from the kitchen startled her and she thrust the paper into her tunic pocket. She stuck her head out. "Who's there?"

"No one!" Obun froze, wide-eyed, by the table with a bread roll.

"Don't worry, sprout, I won't tell," she said. "You need more food than you're getting."

"Thanks," he breathed, then put the bread in his pocket and loped outside.

That was her good deed for the day. She wiped and replaced the shelf contents in a happier mood.

Once the cleaning was done, she locked up and left; she'd be back before them. Danel was waiting for her, as arranged, by the prezzel cart in Ironmongers Alley. The street was as narrow as a debt servant's bed, and reeked of the forge, but it was one place Marel and her tattlers wouldn't come looking. She paused at the corner, watching as he paid for two salted prezzels, chatting with the cart girl. His fine golden hair brushed his shoulders, which were more suited to a blacksmith than a dyemaker. He'd worked his parents' farm until he was fifteen. When the flu took them, he'd just started apprenticeship, and worked every spare hour hauling timber to support his younger brother and sister. Fortunately, they were now apprenticed and he'd taken over the dyeworks last year. His outfit was sky-blue, both the color of his eyes and an allowable extravagance as it displayed his work. Rya blessed the day Marel sent her to get a tunic dyed. The only thing keeping him from perfection were his multi-hued hands, an inevitable drawback of dyemaking.

"Hola, blue boy—is one of them for me?"

He turned and grinned. "You can have both if you're hungry," he said, holding them out.

That stung, but she kept her face blank. His generosity was status-blind, but it hurt to be unable to provide for herself. *Just let me buy myself out, with enough left over for a small loom, and we will astound the town with our goods.* Only not this town—after these humiliating two years, she would never settle down inside these walls. Fortunately, Danel also wanted out, hankering to follow the Pioneer Trail into the wilderness. Rumor said there were cities with good salvage farther east, and the towns forming around them needed crafters. *Soon,* she promised herself. *Soon.* Meanwhile there was this afternoon.

They found a low wall near a horse trough and sat with shoulders touching. Danel was grinning.

"Remember I told you last week traders came through with new powders they swore were ancient dyes?"

"Yes—and were they?"

"At first, they didn't do more than pale pink and yellow. But I played around with mordants and . . ." He fished in his tunic and pulled out two squares of linen. Rya caught her breath—one was red like a hen's comb and the other a glorious orange, like fall lilies.

"Those colors are going to bring you more money than water over a dam!" Rya turned the scraps over and over, marveling. They really *were* old-color!

"That's what I thought," he agreed, grinning. "And it means I could work anywhere—*anywhere*, Rya."

She winced, knowing what he was hinting at. No one would actually stop her from walking out of town, and with a bit of planning, they could be gone before Marel suspected. But her sister, happily married in River Stones, would never be able to see her if she was an outlaw. And Rya's gut clenched at the thought of running from that whore Marel, instead of being legally released. Danel glanced at her and sighed.

"I didn't expect you'd change your mind."

"It's not *absolutely* no. Hold it in reserve. But I don't want you married to a renegade."

He stroked her hand. They'd agreed to put marriage off until they found a new town, though Rya longed to be lying in his bed each night.

"I'm going to pay a scribe to go to the Council office and read my contract, and this time I'll understand what it means. There *must* be a way to do this honorably."

"Well, if you're determined, I recommend Oliv, around the corner from me. She's honest *and* she's discrete."

Rya knew what he meant—this town had more well-paid gossips than a rat had fleas. Keeping one's business private was trickier than standing on a floating log.

"I'll go tomorrow," she said. "I have a tunic-length of linen I can trade."

"If it's not enough—though I'm sure it will be—tell her I'm happy to dye it without cost."

Rya hugged Danel tightly, not wanting him to see her tears. She *couldn't* let the sausage shrew keep her from this relationship. This was her life partner, and no doubt.

"And now, I'd better get back to the parade," Danel said, reluctantly releasing her.

"Are you . . . are you going to that?"

"Have to." He shifted on the bench, looking down. "Have to walk with the guilds."

"Oh. Yes. I forgot." The gap between free and servant yawned like a gully between them. She forced a smile and left quickly, not looking back.

The streets were as crowded as she'd ever seen, both sides of the narrow lanes clogged with rivers of shoving sightseers. Some took the chance of selling unlicensed prepared food, mostly roasted nuts, dried meat or ales. One burly man had a full keg on his back, with a boy tapping the ale. Along the parade route, townsfolk gossiped and enjoyed tumblers, jugglers and musicians. One troupe had erected a tiny stage by the library, a platform with flour-sack curtains. Rya moved closer.

"...and the terrible breath passed through their towns, and they wailed, but no one could escape the poisons released by the new clear wind. Most laid down and died, but some ran into the caves and hid themselves, living as blind moles for years."

A spindly man with gray braids, wearing an indigo robe painted with white stars, gestured wildly as his troop mimed the tale of The Great Sickness. Rya turned away—she'd heard this many times, and it was too sad. But then the troupe began to sing "We Live Together or We Die," one of her favorites. She joined her voice as the song spread through the crowd, though looking around, she noticed she wasn't the only one singing with a wry expression. This motto got short shrift in Cascade Falls.

The actors shifted to a lighthearted story, "The Rabbit and Turtle." One slim girl wore long ears and a silly puffball nose, and a boy carried a battle shield on his back for a shell. The girl loped and bounced around the boy, laughing, dancing a jig, wearing herself out in mockery, and finally lying down by a man in brown trousers holding tree limbs. She pretended sleep, and the boy crept past her, shifted a large "rock" of gray fabric, and ushered out the rest of the troupe dressed as other creatures—a chicken, dog, horse, and lastly, a man. They gathered at the edge of the stage and solemnly recited, "The motto is: 'Slow and steady saves our race.'" Rya had always liked that tale. It reminded of the dangers of progressing too fast and explained why turtles were sacred while rabbits could be hunted. At some point in the past, the turtles had apparently saved everyone.

A pair of guitarists and a drummer took the stage, and started "Turkey in Straw." Rya was swept into a line of dancers, and she jigged and laughed, momentarily forgetting her troubles. This was what life used to be—and would be again, she promised herself.

All too soon, official horns sounded, and parade marshals forced people back. Rya found a wooden box near a wall and climbed it, letting draped fabric nearby conceal her. She didn't want to chance Marel noticing.

The parade snaked around the square: first the militia with leather armor and long pikes; then burghers on horseback—the men with red silk cloaks reaching over the horses' rumps and the women in long colorful gowns with white cloaks trimmed in fur. The cloaks were symbols of office, bought with months of taxes. They were passed down, although *these* burghers had somehow been re-elected so they didn't have to give up the houses, cloaks, fine horses, guards—all the trappings of authority. It wasn't according to Township rules, but no one could—or would—find anything amiss.

After the town officials came the civil servants: teachers, healers, energy and water monitors—each with an embroidered sash indicating seniority and position.

They had comfortable jobs that also didn't pass to others, though expertise in those fields wasn't a bad thing. Next, the rich—those with nothing more to recommend them than property and goods. They were carried in open sedan chairs draped with bright embroidered cloths glinting with jewels. Finally at the tail-end, the craft masters, each with their guild banner: Metalsmiths, Woodturners, Fabricsmiths. She leaned out past the cloths, waved at Danel and smiled as he winked. Next year, she would be among them. *But not here. Somewhere free.*

She breathlessly arrived back just before the household and pretended she'd been cleaning vigorously. Marel was too full of the crowd's cheers to notice. The next day, before she lost her nerve, Rya seized on a shopping errand to visit the scribe.

Oliv's shop was tiny but neat, with a desk, two chairs and a long shelf full of papers and books. The light wood walls held samples of fancy writing; some had flowers and even faces tangled up in it. Rya stood by the door, feeling lower-class compared to the petite, well-dressed elder behind the desk. Oliv had white hair cut below her ears, a slight stoop that caused her pale green tunic to hang lopsided, and she wore those odd pieces of glass that Rya had only seen on clerks at the Council chambers. The old woman smiled and gestured her forward.

"Do you want something written, my dear?"

Rya shook her head as she approached. She held out her fabric. "I would like something read. Specifically, I'd like you to read my . . . my contract of debt service." She blushed. "Rya Greenstone and Marel Quiller, two years ago. There seems to be some confusion. . . ." How much should she tell this woman?

But Oliv nodded shrewdly and said, "I often get such requests. You wouldn't be the first where the contract seemed to favor the other party."

It took Rya a moment to translate "party," but then her eyes widened. "You mean this is common?"

"Too common." The old woman sighed and held out her hands for the cloth. "This is very fine work—it might be an overpayment."

"Oh no. This is important to me and it would—"

"It might not be as useful to you as you think, but we can hope. We can hope." She turned the cloth over and stroked it gently. "This is extraordinary work."

"Thank you. I was much in demand before . . . I had to sell my loom so that my sister could marry a good man. It was worth it." She stopped before she choked up.

"I could take a small piece—or you could pay me from your first length after you set up again."

She was being so nice! Rya was going to cry soon. She shook her head, then remembered the little parchment. Pulling it out, she said, "No—take it all. It is enough for a tunic. But could you also read this for me?"

Oliv spread it on the table. "It's a birth certificate," she said. "*Twin Rocks*

Health Center—that's two towns over—certificate of birth for Obun Quiller, son of Norril Quiller—"

Rya gasped. Obun! He was her *family*!

"A grandchild of Marel's. Interesting. How do you know him? You don't have to answer."

"He—works in the same house. Does it say how old he is?"

Olive glanced down. "He would be eleven at this point."

"I *knew* it! He's too young. Oh, but if he's family . . ."

"Children are allowed to work for their families, yes."

"But she treats him like a dog. He's starved and—" Rya swore under her breath, enraged. "Why would Marel not acknowledge him?"

Oliv shrugged. "A number of reasons—if I'm remembering correctly . . ." She paused, then said, "You might want to ask around about her son. Others can tell you more than I know."

Rya remembered Danel's comment about Oliv's discretion. So she wouldn't get the information from her. But she was pointing in a helpful direction.

"I have to go to the Council chambers today, so I'll read your contract. Come back tomorrow about this time, and I'll let you know what I found."

Rya thanked her repeatedly, and left the shop with a buoyant heart. She'd already been gone too long, so she raced to the market square, looking for the fresh plums Marel wanted. She went up to a fruit stall tended by a muscled terracotta-toned woman, sister to one of the washerwomen. She held out her cloth bag.

"I'll take one of those baskets-full," she said pointing at the plums. "Marel wants some."

"If they're for her, I'm tempted not to sell," the woman grumbled, smiling to show she was joking.

"She's a winter-woke bear, that's for sure," Rya said, then impulsively added, "I heard she even drove her son away." She held her breath.

The woman chuckled. "I remember Norril. She didn't chase him out. He was a spendthrift who 'just happened' to leave town before the Council started investigating some grain missing from a barn of his that'd been rented by a neighbor. No one's heard word of him since."

Rya thanked the woman and headed back. So this Norril had fathered at least one child, who'd come to Marel's. But instead of being pampered, he was being punished—for his father's sin? It was abominable, no matter what.

The rest of the day and through the night, Rya imagined and rejected countless scenarios about her contract. More distracted than usual, she earned scolding not only from Marel but from the cook. It was the longest day she'd ever experienced.

But finally it was almost time. She was helping in the garden, when the smell of smoke drifted across the courtyard, piercing her daydreams. It didn't smell like cookfires—there was a bitter tang that raised an instinctive panic. The gardener raised his head and went to the gate. This had been a dry month, and even by a river, fire was an ever-present fear. The smell got stronger. Rya tensed—was Danel safe?

Marel appeared at the window. "Tad—get up the ladder and start dousing thatch! Rya—find out where!"

Rya raced out the back gate. If danger was low, dare she use the time to visit Oliv? She heard the firecart bell, clearing the way. In Taylors Lane, shopkeepers dragged stuff inside. She followed the crowd, reaching the corner as the firecart clattered past, its huge horses straining against the weight of the waterbarrel. The arms of the pump-rocker allowed four men to pump water through hoses of tight-woven silk sealed with tree sap. The cart was worth two silos of grain, but necessary since buckets were almost useless fighting a large house fire. Even with strict precautions, fire was the town's worst fear. There was a 20-cred reward for reporting careless burning. The Council had been discussing a scheme to augment roof cisterns with aqueducts and channel water via bamboo pipes. It would cut sunlight in areas, but supporters argued a bad fire could destroy the entire town.

Smoke was rising midway down Elm. The crowd gathered with buckets, forming a chain. She realized Danel's shop backed onto this street. Pushing against traffic, she raced around the corner and saw him on the roof, dumping water from his roof-cistern. She hurried around back and called up, then leaped aside as water ran off in sheets, puddling along the patio. It was stupid, this town rule—thatch was *meant* to repel water; only old thatch would retain much. Better to wait and toss water on drifting embers. She climbed the ladder—the fire-struck building was near but not directly behind. Thankfully, smoke and embers blew the other way, but red flame flickering out one window terrified her.

"Here's another reason I want to leave," Danel said, as he straddled the roof. "Everything could go in an hour. Should I pack now, or hope this is contained?"

"You pack and I'll watch for embers," she offered. He frowned, then nodded. He poured water along the crest, scrambled down and handed her the bucket.

"Please be careful."

He raced off and Rya settled herself to watch. The thin stream of pumped water went into the burning window, not doing much. *Damn.* She'd be in trouble for not returning quickly. A gang of boys ran in and scrambled onto boxes to see over the back wall.

"Hola! I'll pay one of you four creds to tell Marel Quiller where the fire is. Half now, half on return."

"What if it's all burned then?" A dirty-faced blond with a wide-brim cap cocked his head and put a hand on his hip.

"It won't be. Here—" She tossed a coin; he caught it expertly. "The pink house on Tucker's Road—tell them I'm helping here."

She resumed watch. Slowly the flames turned to darker smoke and the smell and hiss of wet wood replaced the frightening crackle. Shouting and cheering in the street gave running commentary. Finally it seemed safe to climb down.

Danel emerged from the shop with a length of green wool on his arm. "It's done," she said. "Now you can unpack. Sorry."

"Don't be. I couldn't have done both. You know, we really do make a wonderful team."

"The best," she replied, and kissed him vigorously. "And we're going to make this team permanent. And we're going to do it *soon*."

"If Oliv can help you . . ."

"Oh—she has! She's reading the paper today! She's a gem. I feel *really* hopeful."

"I love you for your strength and your hope," he said.

"And I love you—for *everything*," she said. "I've got to run—Marel will be livid. Meet again, same place on Sunday?" He nodded and she left before she could get too weepy.

She was already late—she might as well grab this chance. She'd never get out again today. She hurried to Oliv's and looked both ways before stepping inside. She didn't want witnesses. Oliv smiled when Rya opened the door—a good sign.

"I think you'll be happy to hear this," she said without preamble. "The contract says that if the time exceeds the agreement, it must be reviewed at Council meeting and the overage explained."

"*Yes*! Thank the Goddess!" Rya danced around the room, then stopped dead. "But Marel's known for her 'gifts' to Council. How do I make sure she doesn't buy them off?"

"Yes, we all know about Marel. But we need to be careful. Let me think about it. We have time. You have a month to request a meeting before it's assumed you agree to continuing."

"I definitely *don't*—but she claims she can extend the time whenever I don't fulfill my service. Like two weeks ago, I was to sew pockets on a tunic, but she suddenly said she needed it immediately, then claimed I hadn't done as she requested, and fined me another two weeks service. Was that fair?"

"Aside from the foul trick, the rules say the fine cannot exceed the time neglected. That means if you slacked off for two hours she could only fine you two hours."

"She's well beyond *that*! But her staff would never give witness. How do I prove she's done this?"

"Why don't you tell me each of the incidents, and I'll write them down. If the others were as excessive, it shouldn't be hard to prove you couldn't have been lazing that long. And remember—if other staff lies for her, they're liable for prison also. Dishonesty was one of the crimes that brought down civilization, books say. That's why lying can only be paid for with prison time."

This woman would get a full outfit of the best dyed linen she and Danel could create!

"Aside from Danel, you're the first one here who wasn't stuck on her own profit."

Oliv replied, "Sadly, I'm not surprised. This town has become too much like the ancient civilizations. When greed poisons one's actions, lying and a cold heart are inevitable. And it cascades like trees blown down in a storm. Before you know it, no one's standing tall."

"And still you stay?" Rya could have bitten her tongue in half for that—how rude, after this woman's kindness!

But Oliv laughed sadly. "I'm too old to begin a strenuous life outside the walls, and I have two children who have two children, who are my heart and keep me here."

"I'm sorry, I didn't—"

Oliv patted her hand. "I like your honesty—it's refreshing. I don't have to read between your lines." She laughed again.

Rya didn't understand, but knew it was a compliment. So for the next half hour, she described the times Marel had accused her of slacking off or breaking something, thus owing more time.

"I believe if there's property damage, one can only lose money. That means you'd leave poorer, but can't be held longer."

"At this point, I'd be happy even if I left naked."

Oliv chortled. "I don't think it'll have to go that far."

Rya stopped by the burnt house. Marel would want details. It stood, but half was blackened, and the whole was drenched, everything inside ruined. She surreptitiously wiped soot on her face and hands to bolster her story. When she returned, the cook said Marel was in the reception hall, ". . . and don't expect much mercy."

Rya sought for a defense. Debt service wasn't slavery—like Oliv said, there *were* rules. She reviewed what she remembered of the terms: no physical punishment, no starvation or withholding sleep. No humiliating tasks.

Marel was holding an ancient globe of that non-ice with a big-eared mouse in red pants "frozen" within. She whirled when Rya entered, but put the globe carefully back before striding forward.

"I gave you an order—and you ignored it! That is deliberate refusal of service!" Her sausage face was suffused with pink and she was shaking; her glare was triumphant. "You owe me another month's service for this!"

"No—I was helping at a town emergency," Rya replied, thinking—*a month for an hour?!?* Now she knew that was illegal. She resisted a smile. "That allows me to temporarily postpone service—*and* I sent someone back to tell you."

"No one came back," Marel said, but her crafty look told Rya she was lying.

"I'll find the boy and he'll speak for me. A lie is punishable by prison, you know."

Marel quickly erased her expression of brief panic, but Rya had seen it. She pressed her luck. "*And* I am demanding a review of my service terms. You agreed to two years and I've done them."

Marel laughed. "No—you are a lazy good-for-nothing and I caught you shirking. The extensions were valid."

"We'll see what the Council says."

"Yes. We will," Marel said, her smile confident.

"You shouldn't have given away your intent," Danel said at the end of week, as they walked along the river. "She has more time to plan now."

"I know—I'm always too hasty." Rya sighed. "But it did distract her from fining me over the fire. I don't want to do a single hour more."

She'd told Danel the good news, and of Oliv's kindness. She also told him about Obun, how poorly he was treated. "I would love to take him with us," she said, squeezing Danel's hand. "But that's probably impossible."

"Who knows? I could use an apprentice." He smiled at her and she kissed him.

"You really are the most amazing man. This debt service is worth all the pain, because I found you here."

Marel did everything possible to keep Rya in the house, to prevent her from organizing her defense. But Marel didn't know about Danel, who was able to relay information to and from Oliv. In a week's time, a plan came together: to report that Marel claimed an additional six months' time for approximately ten hours of infractions and to call as witnesses not only the household servants, but two maids who had been freed last year and who Oliv discovered had more damaging information on Marel.

"Oliv says the best strategy is to present this to Marel in front of witnesses, like Oliv and me, and do what the maids did—demand instant release and full payment in order to prevent a Council meeting," Danel said one evening.

"I don't want her to know about you, until I am absolutely sure this'll work," Rya replied. "It's only because she doesn't that I have any chance at all. Nor do I want her trying to hurt you. She's capable of anything. Look at all the tricky ways she's keeping me close these days." Marel had instructed Rya to do a full count of all clothing and household linens and dictate it to a hastily-hired scribe. She also had made Rya polish every piece of metal jewelry with a special paste and a soft cloth, which took her two days and left her hands aching.

"I can have my brother show up," he replied. "But I think she's right—I don't trust the Council any more than Marel, and if the town hasn't protested yet, they won't speak up. Best to get out from and go."

Rya fumed. "The worst thing about that way is that afterwards she can say whatever she wants about me, and I won't be here to defend myself. It's not just me, it's my family's good name." She saw his face. "But—I will go along with it. I just wish I could bring Obun, too."

"Maybe if she hates him so much . . ."

Rya shook her head. "I doubt it. There's something very dark here. I'm not that important, but he's her grandson—her blood."

Rya was still fuming about it the next day when she noticed Obun trudging to the latrine with a shovel. She impulsively fell in step with him.

"Morning, sprout—another fun job, eh?"

He shrugged. "It gets me away from her."

"How did your parents allow you to work here, anyway?"

"I don't know. I don't remember them." A look of pain crossed his face. Rya mentally kicked herself. "I do remember a sweet lady with brown hair. But I remember big men came and took me away in one of those carried chairs, with the curtains pulled. And then I guess I was here."

"Did Marel ever tell you *why*?"

"Once when I was little and she was in a good mood, she told me I'd been kidnapped and she'd rescued me, and I should be grateful to her for the rest my life."

Rya bit her lip. Kidnapped, yes. Rescued—doubtful.

Obun laughed, but it was an old man sound. "Maybe I would've been better off with those kidnappers."

She patted him on the shoulder. "Don't give up. Sometimes a new life is just around the corner."

Even as the household routine continued, staff became aware that Marel's extra bitter outbursts were due somehow to Rya. For her part, Rya was polite but distant, her mind whirling with plans. She and Danel began arranging their journey, Rya contributing her few coins, Daniel finishing up jobs. The boxes and bags in Danel's back room grew, as did her hope—and fear. She'd never before been so frightened of one person—but she'd never fallen into the hands of a monster before. Her heart bled for the others who might be penned by need; she noticed more frowns and hunched shoulders on her rare trips to town—had they always been there? What *else* was just below the surface?

Despite the restrictions, within two weeks Rya presented Marel with an official notice of Council meeting. She was delighted to see the color drain from Marel's face, and to see her crush the paper in one hand, while striving for a bland expression.

"Do you really think those good men and women will listen to a piece of trash like yourself?" she sneered.

"Every townsmun has the right to be heard, and it's a public forum—won't be just your friends hearing me," Rya replied. "You got greedy, Marel, and you're so far out of bounds now that a child could prove you wrong. Not to mention a number of other indiscretions you *bought into*." Oliv, still being discreet, had helped her frame the accusation in vague but carefully selected terms. Marel paled again—she'd hit some mark.

"However," she said, watching Marel closely, "it's possible that arrangements could be made—in front of witnesses, written down. And I will walk out of that room officially freed."

"Only the Council—" Marel started, but Rya held up her hand.

"A revised claim can be filed in special situations," she said. "I know you can make this a special situation. And I *know* you will want to." She stared at her employer as she might stare down a wild dog. In a moment, Marel flinched and looked away.

"I will sleep on it, and tell you tomorrow," she said and waved her out of the room.

That night, Rya listened to Tyra's breathing beside her in their windowless closet. She reviewed the plans and tried to ignore her heavy gut. If Marel agreed, they'd meet in three days at Oliv's, and Rya would get her release. *If* all went well. Danel suggested moving her things into his house immediately, so she wouldn't have to return. But what would the others, especially Obun, think if she vanished? Marel would put a nasty spin on it, and she would feel like a sneak-thief. She compromised by bringing over her few valuables while leaving trinkets and a change of clothes. She intended to say goodbye and thank each staff, even if they'd acted badly. *They* were crushed by Marel also. Maybe she'd give them hope. But what about Obun? Should she hand him his birth certificate? Could an eleven-year-old keep it safe? She *wanted* to take him, and Oliv agreed to ask, but Rya decided that to let Marel know could hurt Obun worse, if there was any chance he'd have to stay. She had to let it lie.

Even the washday at the river had a bittersweet quality—her last time pounding clothes here, with goddess-grace. The others noticed her quiet, but she just shrugged and said she was tired. She even spared a glance at the tall guard who again teased her with a crude offer. Would she have considered him, if she hadn't met Danel?

When she and Tyra got back, there was no sign of others. Worried, Rya left the basket and hurried inside. Four of the servants were clustered around the door to the reception hall, craning to hear the argument that spilled out.

". . . little thief! Good for nothing but eating my food and sleeping in my stable . . ."

"Obun's in for it now," the cook commented sadly.

"What happened?" Rya whispered.

"Caught stealing an antique. Claims he was only looking at it."

With a sinking heart, Rya listened closer.

". . . sell you to Berl's household! He knows how to keep a worthless servant in line!"

Without thinking, Rya pushed past the group and stepped inside. She squared her shoulders for a fight.

"*One*, you can't sell him because he's not a slave—he's your grandson. Second, *because* he is your grandson, he can't have stolen something that belongs in the family—that's the *rule*. Third, without other grandchildren, he owns *all* this, not just whatever worthless trinket you've got your sausage arms around!"

Marel and Obun stared at her with open mouths. Marel was clutching a palm-sized jewelry box of glinting forest green. Obun had put a table between her and himself, and the welt on his cheek showed she'd already attacked once.

"Wha . . . how dare you—*what* did you say??" Marel rounded on Rya, who stood firm. Her pent-up rage burst out in a great flood.

"I *said* he's your grandson—and you know it damn well. But he doesn't know it, *does* he?"

From the shock on the boy's face, that was true. She continued, "So you treat him like the lowliest servant. Why? To punish him for his father, who was shifty and greedy like you, but not smart enough to get away with it?"

Marel was mute, but rage and panic played across her face. Finally, she spluttered, "You . . . It's all scurrilous lies. You have no proof and I will sell you, too—to the prison maintenance staff!"

A cold point of fear drilled into the rage. *Careful, don't ruin it for both of you.* Taking a deep breath, Rya answered with forced calm, "I *do* have proof, and I'll go to Council—and even your barrels of ale won't save you. The town knows about Norril, and it won't take long to check Twin Rocks—yes, you know the proof is there. Is his mother waiting for him? Does she even know??"

Obun had gone pale, and tears glistened in his eyes. He stared at her, his face full of joy and fear. *Oh please, let me not have given him false hope*, she prayed. But even if his parents were gone, the fact that he by rights owned all or part of this property—much better than wandering with her!

Marel's face took on a crafty expression. "Obun, leave us," she said. "I will speak with you later."

With a glance at Rya, he hurried towards the door. Rya wondered how big the bribe would be. Not that she cared.

"No, Marel. We talk in three days in front of witnesses or it's Council." She turned and followed Obun out the door.

The look of panic, admiration and confusion on the faces of the staff almost sent her into a laughing fit. With roiling emotions, she waved them off.

"Better get back to work *now*," she said. In a moment, the hallway was empty except for Obun, whom she took by the shoulder and steered out the back door.

"We don't have much time," she said. "I have your birth certificate, in a safe place. I only just found it," she said as he opened his mouth. "It's probably safest if you can hide somewhere for the next day. She can't really sell you, but she might try something nasty. Do you know a safe place?"

"There's a little room off the brewery floor. I've hid there before."

She patted him on the shoulder. "Go there now. I'll get word." She watched him race out the back gate. Had she just spoiled everything? Maybe *she* should hide. *No*—she wouldn't give in to fear. Marel had more secrets than a whore's bed, and as thick as she was, she must know she couldn't hurt Rya without others responding.

The cook came to the back door and gestured Rya over.

"Really? Her grandson?" Rya nodded. "That's foul." She paused, then lowered her voice and whispered, "The girl who was freed last year told me Marel sold four carts of ale to the outlanders without telling Council." She tapped her finger to her nose and disappeared back inside.

So that was *one* secret. Why didn't the cook use it, she wondered. But that could wait—she had to get a message to Danel! Tyra was hanging clothes and staring; she ignored her. Rya noticed a hoe against the back gate. She grabbed it and made a show of weeding as close to the gate as she could. Messengers were frequent—she could slip them a cred—

"Marel takes poppy juice every night—gets it from the herbalist even though she's not entitled to."

Rya almost dropped the hoe. She spun around. "Who said that?" she hissed. No one replied, and the yard was empty. Were *ghosts* speaking against Marel now?? But it had sounded like the gardener's voice, pitched very low. She kept hoeing, trying not to seem as rattled as she felt.

Whistling preceded a delivery boy with a tray of flatbread. She stepped out.

"Hola! Could you take a message to the dyemaker? For two cred?"

"Sure, why not?"

"Tell him the weaver has put her foot in it. Meet her at nine bells by the stabler's fountain."

"Weaver—foot—nine bells—fountain. Got it."

She handed him a coin and went back to the yard. She was surprised Marel hadn't come after her by now. Honestly, she was itching to know what *was* going on inside. She winched up a bucket of water and brought it to the kitchen.

Tyra and the hairdresser had their heads together, but broke apart instantly. The cook was studiously ignoring her. Rya poured the water into the large kettle and announced, "For washing." A sudden fear struck: would Marel ransack her room? She walked as deliberately as possible toward the sleeping closet off the pantry. A wave of relief—nothing looked disturbed. Marel would hardly be subtle at this point. To be sure, she reached under the low pallet for her small wooden trinket box. She slowly fingered the contents.

"That was brave of you to stand up for Obun."

The box flew from her hand onto the floor.

"Oh! I'm sorry!" Tyra gasped, and knelt to help gather the trinkets.

"It's all right. Thanks. I just couldn't stand it any longer, I guess."

"I understand—I'm about to explode." She leaned closer and lowered her voice. "Berl paid Marel to dispose of some ballots last year. I had to burn them in the grate."

Rya gasped, then thanked her. *Now* what?? Could she walk out, leaving all of these dirty secrets? With a sinking heart, she realized her greed to escape had almost caused *her* to cheat—not as bad as Marel, but it was a slick slope. Tears welled up. Why her??

That night she told Danel, "I can't make the deal. This place is as rotten as an old board—it'll kill someone, soon!"

Danel stared at her, his face mirroring the intense pain, hope and fear she had passed through that afternoon. So close—but . . . at what cost? Twice he opened his mouth to speak, then shut it. Rya watched anxiously. He groaned softly, rubbed his face, then straightened up. "You're right. Clean start or none. I'll tell Oliv tomorrow." He smiled, though his eyes were agonized.

Any doubts she'd had about the partnership vanished at that moment. She kissed him tenderly. If this went wrong, they could both be thrown in prison, accused of lying. But they'd face this together; his strength shoring up hers.

‡‡

Marel was amazingly well-behaved the next few days. *She must be terrified,* Rya thought. The days felt unreal, and Rya jumped at shadows. Fearing to lead Marel to her friends, she waited. She got a message from Oliv: Obun was safe and Oliv was preparing a child abuse case for Council. Danel sent a tantalizing message: "Board breaking. Safe landing hopeful."

Then news broke all over town—the market was buzzing, the cook reported. Marel had gone to the Council and accused Berl of burning ballots, saying she'd been blackmailed into cooperating. Hearing her claims pushed townsfolk to speak out—the woman with the ale-cart tale, a man who falsified notes at Council, and Michel the yardman, who accused Marel of stealing old-color salvage and selling it in Twin Rocks through her son. He led them to a room of old-color trinkets at her home, and the owners were reportedly calling for her execution.

The uproar stopped everything for a while. When Marel was arrested, Rya was finally able to go to town. She and Danel met Oliv, to decide how much they would tell Council.

"I can testify about the certificate, but I only know the story from Obun. Will he have to talk?" Rya asked.

"I'm not sure," Oliv replied. "My children are researching in nearby towns. We're looking for adults who knew."

"My case of debt-fraud seems petty now."

"And yet important. Would other staff talk?"

"Cook says she'd actually *been* freed, but had nowhere else to go. Tyra might—she says she's seen papers in hidden locations."

"Every bit is important. If one accusation fails, another will stick. The Council is debating a proposal to search Marel's house." Oliv patted Rya's shoulder. "We have a lot to thank you for."

"Me?? I just wanted to get free . . ."

"But you stood up to her. I once said greed spreads like falling timber. Now it seems courage does, too. And some rotten timber might be falling soon."

The past days' events *did* feel like a house, or a prison, collapsing—the dust flying, barriers vanishing. Rya could suddenly picture walking out of the town gate with Danel, their belongings carted and ready to set up in a new town, a freer place.

". . . but I suppose nothing's guaranteed," she murmured, unaware she'd said it aloud until Danel answered.

Danel put his arm around her. "With your courage, we won't have to worry about anything we meet on the way."

She leaned her head on his chest. "My courage comes from your love, and the caring of others." She smiled at Oliv. "We'll find a way to stay in contact. These town walls choke off the heartblood of the people."

Oliv nodded. "It's time to discuss that in Council. What are we protecting, what are we hiding? Our real wealth is in people. Time we realized that."

Look for Catherine McGuire's new
deindustrial science fiction novel, *Lifeline*,
coming this winter from Founders House Publishing.

Learn more at cathymcguire.com

The Prisoner of Genda
by Matthew Griffiths

SET IN THE WORLD OF
STAR'S REACH by John Michael Greer

The Prisoner

Cold sweat chilled the back of his neck. His breath came in shallow gasps and hung silver in the frigid air. With a grunt, he hefted the pole against the town wall, and then turned it so the foot holds he had notched faced outward.

His eyes lifted to the curved quarter moon that hung low in the black sky. A grey cloud drifted across and its rim glowed briefly before blocking the moonlight.

He grasped the pole and clambered up to the top of the wall. He steadied himself, pulled the pole up to vertical then shoved it into the darkness so it fell lengthways along the base of the wall. Hopefully no one would notice and raise the alarm for a few days at least. That was all he would need.

The stink of pigs rose to his left and stung his nostrils. To his right a dark smudge of smoke rose into the sky and bent lazily to the south. He had dragged his crude ladder a few meedas further away from the house. Far enough, he hoped, to avoid the greenhouse and, with luck, land on the compost heap.

He couldn't be sure. Even in three years the town had changed. The wall was enlarged to the west and on the east side a new gate had been constructed facing the road to the city. He wondered how his family further north were faring. He hoped they too had prospered, but he didn't plan to stay, even if he could. A short visit under cover of darkness would be all.

He patted the breast pocket of his heavy fur coat and mumbled a prayer.

Then he leapt into the darkness.

The crash of glass shattered the silence and sharp edges scratched at him. He landed heavily on the ground in a shower of shards.

"Sackemon!"

He rolled to a halt amongst some low plants. A rivulet of blood began to ooze from the back of his neck. His eyes strained to make out the door. He stood gingerly and felt his way along the thick stone wall at the rear of the greenhouse. It was warm as it released the heat from the day's wintery sun.

A shaft of light swung across the glass above him and he heard running boots thump on the earth outside. He slunk into the deep shadow in the corner of the greenhouse. The door creaked open just a few meedas away. A short gleaming barrel poked through the gap illuminated by a swaying lantern, followed slowly by a cautious face and then two figures in thick red jackets.

Sackemon, Mounties.

"Gotcha! Raise your hands where we can see them."

He looked up and winced as the lantern glare seared his eyes. He shaded his face with both hands and squinted at the men. Two Mounties. Faces almost as red as their coats. He smelled beer on their breath. Off duty, on the way home. He shook his head. Bad luck or not, he was too close to give up now.

"Get up."

He half rose, staggered and fell sideways into the plants.

"Get up. No funny business."

He rose slowly, arms raised, then rolled right, threw a fistful of dirt at the Mountie with the gun and ran for the door.

The lantern bobbled. "Get him!" A truncheon blow landed on his head and he fell to the ground again. The Mountie with the gun pointed it at his face, unwavering. "Stand up, hands on your head and don't move a senamee."

The prisoner slowly got to his feet, shielding his eyes from the light.

"Check his pockets."

The other Mountie handed over the lantern. Stepping behind the prisoner, he removed a knife and a small tomahawk slung from the prisoner's wide leather belt, setting them aside. Then he reached into the coat pockets and smiled as he raised a small clinking bag of coins, weighing it in his hand. "Just reward for a hard night's work, eh?"

The other Mountie grinned. The money bag disappeared into a red pocket and the Mountie patted down the prisoner's legs. "That's it." He picked up the knife and tomahawk and raised them to the light. "Navy issue knife." He looked again at the prisoner, still shielding his eyes. "Looks like we might have ourselves a deserter."

The other nodded. "His coat looks Rosh made." He pushed aside the prisoner's hands and stared at his face. "On the run, are we?" The prisoner jerked his head away and said nothing.

The Mountie shrugged. "Let's get him to the pokey." He kicked the prisoner's leg. "Get movin'. Jail's the only place you're going tonight."

THE WIDOW

A loud voice rang out over the hubbub of the busy tavern. "Quiet down now, it's time." The chatter in the room stilled. A tar player in one corner continued to strum but was quickly silenced by an icy stare from the hard faced woman at the bar. She turned and adjusted the volume on the radio.

"Today the Meer of Genda, heronna Magg Winn the fourth, has announced that next year, the thirtieth of her gummint, will be celebrated by a grand tour. She will visit cities, towns and hamlets throughout the country to meet the people and preside over ceremonies to inaugurate suitable memorials and monuments. The itinerary will be selected by a juree of citizens and ministers. All munees of Genda are invited to put forward their proposals for consideration."

Hushed voices immediately began discussing this exciting new development and the chances of the town of South Foray getting on the Meer's itinerary, off the main road as it was, west of Otwa.

"Pipe down!" the woman at the bar shouted.

"In the north, the Genda navy yesterday intercepted and repelled an Arab pirate raid off the coast of Greenlun."

Rouss darra Sage's ears pricked up and her eyes flitted to the brown wooden box in the corner where the disembodied voice continued. "The Genda forces suffered no casualties in the action." She exhaled and continued wiping down the bar. She wore a loose black blouse buttoned to the neck, decorated only by a small wooden cross hung on a smooth leather cord and wisps of deep auburn hair that escaped her bun.

A man entered the tavern and closed the door. He turned and removed his hat, eyes searching the room. Finding what he was looking for, he strode toward the end of the bar. He stopped in front of the black clad woman, wrestling the hat in his grip. "Rouss darra Sage," he whispered. "My wife's pains have started. She asks that you come."

The woman eyed him warily with her green eyes, one finger slowly lifting to touch the cross at her throat. "Are you sure it's me she wants?"

He nodded rapidly several times. "Yes, please come. You delivered her sister's baby and she gives thanks to Mam Gaia every day for your help."

"What of sister Fauney?"

"She is away, visiting the city temple. And anyway my wife asks for you."

"I will need to go home first and get my bag." The man nodded. She turned and whispered to the young brown haired woman beside her. "Tarshay, I have to go." She took off the money pouch tied around her waist and handed it to her. Rouss nodded to the woman behind the bar, who nodded in return and then leaned closer to the radio.

"The gummint announced today that development of the northern territories will increase this summer. Three new settlement areas will be opened to citizens. Further details will be announced in due course. The Minister of Guilds and Merchandise Trade also welcomed growing exchanges with our southern neighbours Meriga and Meyco . . ."

THE PRENTICE

Three sharp raps on the door jolted Rouss awake. She brushed her hair from her pale face and glanced at the window. Light crept in around the edge of the heavy curtain. "Who is it?" she called.

"Prentice Tagair, Mam. Mister Bartim sent me to do some more work on your roof."

She groaned and pulled back the covers, swung her feet onto the cold floor. She felt for her slippers and slid her feet inside. Padding to the door, she pulled her coat on over her night dress and slid back the bolt. As the door opened she shivered in the frosty air.

A young man stood there clad in a fur hat, leathers and jacket, wearing a tool belt and carrying several lengths of wood over his shoulder. "I told him the roof was fine. A little sagging doesn't matter."

"Yes Mam, I know, but he insisted." He put the wood down in front of the mulch covered herb garden beside the worn stone doorstep.

"You must be just about due to be a Mister yourself?"

He stood a little straighter. "Yes Mam, next summer." Then he sagged. "If Mister will let me. He says I'm not ready."

"Is that so?"

He shrugged, then looked up and down the lane and lowered his voice. "Can I ask you something?"

"Yes, of course."

"I've been thinking, since I'm soon to be a Mister and I have a little money saved and . . ."

Her eyebrows lifted and her lips curved with amusement. "And since you've had your eye on a certain young woman for longer than I can remember?" His face reddened and he looked down. "I've see the way you look when you talk with her in the tavern."

He raised his eyes to hers. "Do you think . . . does she . . . would she?"

She smiled and tucked a lock of red hair behind her ear. "I think it's time you had a serious talk with her."

"But . . ." His face twisted in anguish. "I never know what to say, apart from the weather and the news. What I really want to say is how her laugh sounds like a songbird in spring and her freckles are like drops of sunlight on her skin."

Rouss laughed. "That would be a good start. Maybe it's also time to tell her about your plans and find out what hers are?"

He bit his lip and nodded. "There is another complication."

She pursed her lips. "Her father?"

He nodded.

"I think it is time I had a chat to your Mister Bartim about several important matters."

He fidgeted on the doorstep. "Can I start on the roof now?"

She sighed. "All right then, go ahead."

THE GARDENER

"Hallo?" The Mountie shouted, loud enough to be heard three lanes away. "Garint sunna Jardin?"

Garint rounded the corner of the house, his left leg dragging as he limped toward him. A broad grin creased his face through his beard. "Morning. I was in the greenhouse looking at the damage. I'm glad it wasn't me who fell through that glass." His ears stuck out through his unruly hair. He wiped his hands on his rumpled, dirt stained pants.

"We want you to come and have a look at the prisoner. If you know him it might help explain what he was up to."

Garint nodded. "Hang on, I have something to deliver on the way." He ducked into the small house and emerged with a burlap bag tied loosely at the top with twine.

As they walked toward the jail the Mountie prattled on. "Strange fellow, this one. Wears Rosh clothes and carries a Genda navy knife. We reckon he's a deserter. Wouldn't say a word when we nabbed him. He understands though, you can tell it in his eyes."

A distant sound of banging grew louder as they approached a small home with a hammering builder's prentice perched on its roof. Garint asked the Mountie to wait as he went to Rouss's cottage and knocked on the door. She opened it with a smile. "Morning, Garint sunna Jardin!" She shouted to be heard over the din and wiped flour from her hands on an apron.

Garint blushed slightly and smiled. "Morning. Some vegetables for you."

"Thank you Garint. I'll return your book tomorrow with a loaf of bread. I'm busy today," she said, pointing to the builder's prentice hammering in a nail above them.

Garint waved goodbye and rejoined the Mountie. They reached the jailhouse and followed the jailer's slow heavy footsteps down the dim narrow corridor to the cells. The other Mountie waited by the door. The jailer jangled his ring of keys with a flourish and rattled one in the lock. The prisoner looked up from where he lay on the narrow bed, huddled under a rough woollen blanket.

"Get up," said the Mountie. "This is the man whose glass you broke. That kind of salvage is expensive and hard to replace."

Garint took one step forward through the doorway.

"Do you recognise him?" asked the Mountie.

Garint watched carefully as the man dropped his feet to the floor and stood up, head still lowered and all but his bearded face covered by his hat.

"Well?"

The prisoner lifted his eyes for a split second and shivered, ending with the barest shake of his head.

Garint frowned, licked his lips slowly, then shook his head. "He doesn't look familiar."

The Mountie stepped into the room beside him, slapping his wooden truncheon rhythmically into the palm of his hand. "What have you got to say for yourself?"

The prisoner coughed and took a breath. A deep voice resonated from his throat. It reminded Garint of the Rosh baritones he had heard singing on the radio. "I'm sorry about your glass, Mister. I meant no harm. I hope I am able to make amends." He paused, then added with a deliberate slowness, "Please check the soil very carefully for glass."

The Mountie raised his truncheon. "It should be you on your hands and knees in the dirt doing that, you bucket of pig swill."

The other laid a hand on his arm. "Leave him. That's enough for now." He motioned Garint out of the room. "The judge comes to town next week. You will be asked to describe the damage and estimate the cost to replace the glass. You might have to travel to the city for that eh? The judge might also order amends."

The jailer locked the door and replaced the keys on his belt. He looked into the room through the small barred opening in the heavy wooden door. The prisoner's breakfast, a slab of bread with a smear of butter, was only half eaten. A broad smile creased the jailer's face. "Not hungry, eh? What were you expecting, coffee and crussins? Pancakes and maypa sirp? This ain't some fancy Otwa hotel." He turned and shambled away, chortling at his own joke. "Coffee and crussins. Ha!"

THE BUILDER

Rouss darra Sage chatted quietly behind the bar with Tarshay as they tidied up after the lunch crowd. The patrons had thinned out already as people decided they had better do something useful with what remained of their day since half the morning had been spent in a hastily called town meeting.

In the corner, in his usual seat, Mister Bartim leaned back on his chair watching her. Rouss glanced at him out of the corner of her eye. He still wore a formal jacket from the morning's town meeting, which gave his stern face a certain elegance. He needed to smile more. Of course, if she was honest with herself, she had to admit he wasn't the only one. Perhaps he wouldn't make too bad a husband. She felt her face flush at the idea. She looked at the frayed cuffs of her blouse. Oh Leymo, you went off to find adventure and bring back money for our future, and look at me now.

Bartim raised his hand and beckoned her, "Rouss darra Sage, come and sit with me a minute. I'd like to talk with you."

She folded the dish cloth on the bar, winked at Tarshay beside her, and then walked over to him. "Eldmin and Mister." He nodded as she pulled out a chair and sat facing him across the solid wooden table. To his left a chess board sat, its pieces standing to attention, ready for play. An empty beer mug rested between his hands. She sat upright and rested her hands in her lap. "It so happens I have some things I want to discuss with you too."

"I'm pleased." He smiled. "You look lovely as always, although a little colour in your clothing would suit you better."

Rouss responded with a tight smile. She noticed that his jacket enfolded his broad frame a little too tightly, spoiling the effect a little. "I heard the town meeting this morning was interesting?"

Bartim shook his head. "A kerfuffle as usual. Wardin Lormah thinks he can convince people of anything as long as he lets them vent. And he thinks it keeps the Gaian Eldmin happy to ask the questions too. In my view it's better to give people two options you can live with and have them exhaust each other fighting amongst themselves."

"Tarshay tells me there were some good suggestions."

"Hrumpf. Planting in the wastelands? None of us will be around long enough to see any benefit from that."

"Reclothing Mam Gaia for our children and grandchildren is no waste."

Bartim touched the cross at his neck. "Building a monument would be more appropriate for the Meer. A fitting legacy."

"And more lucrative for the builder." A smile tugged at her lips. "I took you for a more public spirited individual, Eldmin Bartim."

Bartim's brows lowered and he suppressed a look of irritation.

"I thought the library idea was a good one too," said Rouss. "There are lots of books that people would benefit from."

Bartim grimaced. "Your friend Garint outdid himself with that one. 'Books are a gift from our ancestors,' he said. You should have seen Eldmin Terrea's face. She went pale as a ghost. The Gaians are as touchy as our church when it comes to old books." He shrugged. "I like the Wardin's idea of a commemorative arch. I've always wanted to build one of those. But I'll be happy to create whatever the council decides."

"If you win the commission of course."

"Of course." He waved a hand in the air. "Anyway that's not what I want to talk about." Bartim pushed the empty mug aside and spread his hands on the table. "It's been some time since we last spoke Rouss darra Sage. I am curious to know your thoughts." He eyed her closely but she displayed no reaction. "I am a widower, you are a widow. We have both experienced the grief of losing a child. We understand each other."

Rouss felt her chest tighten and she struggled to breathe. It was four years ago now, yet it still had the power to twist her insides into knots. Seeing one's own flesh and blood emerge lifeless into the world was an anguish she would not wish upon the vilest creature on Mam Gaia's round belly.

Bartim continued. "My daughter is nearly grown. We can have another child and make a new family together. Have you decided yet to accept my proposal?"

She held her breath momentarily then shook her head slightly as she exhaled. "I have told you Mister Bartim. I cannot make such a decision until I know for sure what happened to my husband."

"It's been several years, Rouss. Your mourning is excessive. Many people think so."

"I do not live my life based on what other people think."

He nodded. "Indeed, and that is an admirable quality. All the same, it's time to let go of the past and build a new life. I'm offering you a fine home—" he smiled "—with a roof that doesn't leak, a secure future . . ."

"I will give you an answer, Mister Bartim, when I feel clearer about my situation." She took a breath. "Right now I have a few other things I would like to talk about."

He sat back with a sigh and rested his hands on the table. "Very well, please speak your mind."

"Firstly, while I appreciate your concern and generosity, there is no need to have prentice Tagair come and fix things at my cottage."

He waved one hand in the air. "It's nothing. Things are slow this winter. He needs something to do. Idle hands make for the devils' work, yes?"

"He is old enough to look after himself. He's almost ready to be a Mister, is he not?"

"In a year or two perhaps."

"Why the delay? Is it for his benefit or yours?"

"In my judgement he's not ready." Bartim smiled thinly. "Although I do concede that he is more useful to me than all my junior prentices put together."

Rouss forced her jaws to unclench and spoke softly. "There is also the matter of the young woman he . . ."

Bartim's hand slammed down on the table. "No. I will most certainly not allow him to marry her. She's too young and he is . . ." He dropped his voice. "He is not suitable."

Rouss leaned forward over the table and hissed, "Is that your judgement talking or something else entirely? You cannot treat people like—" she motioned toward the chessboard "—like pawns in a game."

His face flushed and his eyes narrowed. He took a breath and stared at his rough hands. Finally he spoke. "Rouss darra Sage, I am concerned for her welfare, as I'm sure you can understand. I feel she has missed the guidance of her mother and lacks the necessary . . ." he paused and raised his eyes to hers ". . . judgement in such matters. It is partly my fault. I regret allowing her to work here with my sister-in-law. Too many unsavoury characters."

Rouss dropped her gaze and bit her lip to repress a smile. Bartim caught the glint in her eye. "You would not think it so amusing if she were your daughter I'm sure." He glowered at the table then brightened a little. "Well now. Perhaps that is a solution to all our disagreements. If you were to become her step-mother to keep an eye on her I could consider allowing Tagair to court her, and then, in time, consider a marriage." He raised an eyebrow. "What do you say?"

Rouss darra Sage's mouth tightened. "I understand your protectiveness but if you are reluctant to train up a new senior prentice, how can you commit to a marriage and raising another child? And 'in time' both your daughter and your prentice will do as they wish, if you continue to be unreasonable." She stood up abruptly, the chair scraping on the boards. "Good day."

"Please think about it, Rouss darra Sage. Neither of us can wait forever." He watched her weave through the empty tables, grab her coat from a peg on the wall and slam the door on her way out. He scowled and looked over to the bar where Tarshay stood, head down, arranging mugs behind the counter. The clock still said it was early but he decided he didn't care. "Daughter!" he called. "My mug is empty."

Rouss left the tavern and strode towards her cottage. At a cross road she hesitated, then turned north. The arched church door was propped slightly ajar with a smooth round stone. She slipped inside, knelt briefly in the aisle and sat down in a pew near the back. Rouss sat with her eyes closed and tried to calm herself, seeking some clarity over her tangled thoughts: Leymo gone three years, Bartim's proposal. She had played the role of the grieving widow willingly and with all her heart, all the time hoping he would return. But here, now, she found no solace, nor strength, nor clarity in her feelings. Except the growing awareness that change could not be delayed forever.

Several women sat in the front pews. One glanced around and nudged the woman next to her. "Look, it's the black widow," she whispered loudly. "Praying for her ghost to return."

"I heard she's turning Gaian," the other replied. "That's why half the believers in town won't use her as a midwife."

"I wouldn't neither if it were me."

"You silly fool. We're both too old to be bothered with all that nonsense." They both tittered.

Rouss waited silently for what seemed like an age, ears burning and face set in a scowl. When she decided she had stayed long enough, she abruptly rose to her feet and left.

THE MESSENGER

Tarshay knocked on the jailhouse door. "Come in," said the jailer, not bothering to get up. She opened the door with one hand and light spilled out onto the dark cobbles. She entered balancing a tray and nodded to him. "Dinner for hizonna."

"Very funny," he muttered and continued to scowl at the bulky radio in front of him on the table as he twiddled the dials with his stubby fingers. Behind him a dishevelled bed stood against the far wall under a small curtained window. She transferred a heaped plate of meat and vegetables and a large mug of beer from her tray to the table.

"And the prisoner? Vegetable soup tonight."

"Too good for the likes of him." The jailer jerked his head toward the corridor. "Cell two."

She walked slowly down the corridor, peeked in the window at the man lying on the bench, then placed the bowl on the floor and knelt to unbolt the food hatch. The prisoner jerked awake at the sound. She slid the food inside and closed the hatch. The prisoner leapt up and stood by the door.

"Thank you sister," he said loudly. Then he whispered, "Stay a moment. I have a message for Garint sunna Jardin."

She shrunk back from the door, eyes wide, whites glowing in the gloom.

"Lock the bolt. I mean you no harm. I want you to deliver a message, that's all." He took a half step back. "Please, I beg you this one favour."

She crouched down and bolted the food hatch, then stood up by the small barred window. "What is your message?" she whispered, glancing down the corridor to where the jailer's radio warbled, accompanied by the discordant clang of his fork on the plate.

"I will ask Garint sunna Jardin to come here tomorrow to discuss amends. Ask him to bring some things for me when he comes. It is very important."

She shrunk back again. "You mean to escape."

"No. You know Garint would not help anyone do such a thing."

She hesitated for a moment, then nodded and swept a lock of brown hair from her eyes with a freckled hand. "What things?"

He whispered his message quickly through the bars, then she departed.

Marin's stomach rumbled. He picked up the bowl and slab of bread, murmured a blessing on Mam Gaia and devoured the meal like a starving man who had suddenly been admitted to a feast.

Rouss sat on her bed. Her chest heaved beneath her black blouse and sobs erupted from her throat. Each time her eyes dried she picked up the letter and read it again, until the tears flowed once more. Finally she felt able to get up and make herself a late supper. When she read the letter again afterwards she found her eyes could at last stay dry. Leymo sunna Seena had died at sea as she had been told. Marin had found a sailor at an outpost in Greenlun who was on the ship with him when it went down.

And now Marin was finally back but for some reason couldn't come in person. What could have kept him? Rouss emptied out her mug of cold tea. Outside the window the bulging curve of the moon hung suspended like a beacon over the town. She held the letter tight to her chest and whispered. "A blessing on your dreams Marin sunna Elevar."

A wave of relief swept over her and brought new tears to her eyes. It was followed by a chill wind of shame. She had loved Leymo and hoped day after day for his return for three years. Why then did it feel like she had been released from a huge burden?

THE JAILER

Morning sun slanted in through the open jail house door. The jailer stood by his table, legs spread to support his bulk, and shrugged apologetically. "Rules say I have to check your pockets before you can visit a prisoner." Garint nodded and raised his arms. The jailer's hand snaked into one pocket and withdrew a well-thumbed book. "Still reading enough for the rest of us put together, eh?"

He replaced it and his pudgy fingers fished in another pocket.

"Well, well. What have we here? A mirror!" His yellowed teeth grinned. "It seems Gimpy Garint has decided to spruce himself up today. Now why would that be?" He rubbed his stubbled chin in an exaggerated mime of thoughtfulness. "It's not Semba so it can't be Nowell. No, you're Gaian anyway, but the Solstice has already gone too. Hmmm." He stroked his chin again. "Well then, I reckon it can only be one thing." His mouth curved in a sly grin. "And just who is the lucky lady?"

Garint's cheeks flushed red. "No. I . . ."

The jailer laughed and clapped him on the back with a meaty paw. "It'll be our secret, eh? Just be sure to let me know first. It's not often I get to hear real gossip before everyone else."

The jailer turned and jangled the ring of keys. "Come on. I'll take you to him. Amends is the least of his problems I reckon, if he's a deserter. Yell if you need help."

"I'll be fine. I know how to use these." Garint held up his fists and flashed a lopsided grin.

The prisoner stood by the door and waited until the jailer's footsteps had retreated along the corridor. He turned and whispered. "Did you find the letter? And deliver it?"

"Yes. I put it under her door yesterday. She was out."

"Any reply from her?"

Garint shook his head. "No. I didn't see her this morning. I came straight here when I got your message."

Marin frowned, then looked Garint in the eye. "Sorry about the glass. I was aiming for the compost heap."

Garint grinned. "You only missed by a few meedas. The compost heap is in the same place—in fact, I made it bigger. I also built another greenhouse last winter and you managed to hit that instead. Winter vegetables bring in good money until the frosts leave the fields outside the walls in spring."

Marin nodded. "Things are going well for you cousin. I'm glad. Now it's time for me to make a fresh start." Garint eyed him curiously but he abruptly changed tack. "How is your father?"

Garint dropped his gaze. "He returned to Mam Gaia last winter. A flu got into his lungs."

"I'm sorry." He paused. "Any news from my family?"

"They were in good health last I heard."

He nodded and put an eye to the barred window again and squinted down the gloomy corridor. "Did you bring the things I asked?"

"Yes."

"Good. Take off your clothes."

Garint froze. Marin's gaze pierced him. "I must see her, cousin. You know how I feel about her. I will be back for you as soon as I can. I promise."

Garint's eyes narrowed, then he nodded slowly. "Leymo?"

Marin shook his head. They exchanged clothes and Marin pulled a shard of glass from beneath the thin straw mattress on the bed and used the mirror to trim his beard to a similar length to Garint's. "Did you look after her as I asked cousin?"

"Yes. I gave her vegetables and loaned her books and built a big window ledge inside for her herbs."

"Thank you for that." He continued his rough trimming. "Have you found someone to share your house?"

Garint shook his head.

Marin shrugged. "Maybe just as well, with that leg. That is not something you want to pass on to the next generation."

Garint scowled. "My leg is not a mutation. Father said my big head got stuck coming out when I was a baby is all. I can have healthy children."

"If someone will have you."

Down the corridor the jailer's chair creaked. "Are you alright in there Garint?" he called.

Garint cast a look at Marin. "Yes. Just another minute or two."

Marin spat on the handkerchief from Garint's coat pocket, wiped some of the dirt off his face. "How do I look?"

"A spitting image," said Garint, through clenched teeth.

Marin grinned and grasped his shoulder. "They all said we looked alike enough to be twins when we were young. We will find out if it's still true."

Garint pulled on the Rosh overcoat and the fur hat.

Marin smiled. "Good. You look just like a prosperous Rosh merchant . . . who has perhaps fallen on hard times." He chuckled. "I spend most of my time lying on the bench under the blanket so you can do the same to avoid them seeing your face. If you have to send a message, tell the young woman who brings the food. Just pretend you're me." He pulled Garint's hat low down his forehead and let the flaps drop down on each side of his head. "Is the sunwater tank at your house full? I can't remember the last time I had a bath."

Garint nodded.

"Good. Now, call him like you're in a hurry to go home to your greenhouses."

Garint shouted out to the jailer, then lay down on the bed and pulled the blanket over his head. "Don't forget to limp," he hissed.

The jailer waved Marin through the door. "Remember to tell me all about this mysterious woman, eh?" he said, but received only a grunt in reply.

THE ADVENTURER

Marin stood at the door in the dim light of the early evening, stomach churning. He slowly raised his hand and tapped on the door, then took a step back and removed his hat. The few seconds it took before he heard the bolt drawn back seemed like an age.

"Marin sunna Elevar! Come in!" Rouss pulled him inside and threw her arms around his neck. "Marin, thank you so much for your letter. You have lifted a great weight from my heart." She released her grip, stood back and gazed at his face. "You are a true friend. Leymo sunna Seena would be very pleased today."

Marin took a deep breath. "I did what I had to do."

Rouss waved him to a chair. "I feared you would not return like Leymo. Let me make you some tea." She put the kettle over the fire and bustled around the kitchen bench as Marin sat and watched. She chatted happily, filling him in on all the news he had missed. She finally placed two mugs of tea on the table and sat down. "I can't stop smiling. It's so good to see you."

He cradled the hot mug in his hands. "I am glad to see you too, Rouss. Very glad." He smiled. "How have you been?"

She exhaled a deep breath. "It has been a difficult time, Marin, but I think things will be better now that I know what happened." Now that she no longer had to wait for someone who was never coming back. Her breath caught in her throat and she closed her eyes to fight back the tears.

He nodded and gently squeezed her shoulder while she gathered herself. Then he released his grip and stared at his tea. "Rouss, I have something else to tell you." He bit his lip. "A confession of sorts."

She looked at him keenly, auburn eyebrows raised.

"I didn't do what I did for Leymo. At least not all of it. I did it for you, and myself." His eyes pleaded with her for understanding. "Rouss, I have loved you since I first met you, even before you married him, but I could not say a word to you then, nor since, not until now."

Rouss's gaze was riveted on his face. "What are you saying?"

"I can't stay here," he said, waving his hand in the direction of the town centre. "But that is not such a bad thing." He cast a glance at the fire. "I had to come and tell you what happened to Leymo in person, and tell you how I feel. But they wouldn't let me go so I jumped ship in Rosh and worked my way back here in disguise."

Rouss pursed her lips.

"There is so much more outside these walls. Come with me to the north, Rouss. There are fantastic opportunities there, land for the taking." He paused and pulled a book out of his coat pocket. "Have you read this book of Garint's? It talks of all the things going on there now that the ice has retreated. It's not fantasy, it's real. I've seen it."

"I've read the book." She shook her head. "Are you sure it is not just repeating the mistakes of the past? The spread of people from one end of Mam Gaia's round belly to the other ended in hardship for all her children. Perhaps we should leave her to heal herself without our meddling?"

"Mam Gaia has changed. Why not use it to our advantage? There is plenty of room for all her creatures." He took her hand and enclosed it in his own. "We can make a new life, Rouss, something great for ourselves and our children. I have money saved. I buried it in the forest to the east for safe keeping."

She pulled her hand away and pushed a lock of hair from her face. "Marin sunna Elevar, I don't know what to say. I have always regarded you as a brother, as did Leymo." She stood and walked to the fireplace, hands clasped tightly in front of her. She stared into the flickering flames for several minutes. Marin watched her gravely. His throat constricted so he could not take even a sip of the tea. At last she turned and spoke. "Marin. This is all so unexpected. I need time to work out what I truly feel."

His worked his jaw and swallowed. "It will be a great opportunity for both of us, Rouss. Trust me."

She looked at him closely. "Those are Garint's clothes." Marin nodded. Her eyes widened. "People said a stranger was caught climbing the wall two nights ago, at Garint's greenhouse. That he is a prisoner in the town jail."

Marin nodded. "That was me."

"How did you get out?"

"Garint helped me."

"How? Where is he?" she demanded.

Marin raised his eyes to hers reluctantly. "He is in my cell. We swapped clothes. We have always looked alike, apart from the leg. I got the girl who delivers the food to give him a message."

"You can't leave him there!"

"I would never do that. I will go back and swap with him again once we have made our plans. Then I will work out some way to get free if the judge decides not to be lenient."

Rouss paced the floor. "The young woman with the food. Did she have brown hair and freckles?"

"Yes. I think so."

Rouss shook her head. "You are lucky we are not all behind bars. She is an Eldmin's daughter."

Marin blinked. "I didn't know. She was reluctant at first but I convinced her I meant no harm."

"We must get Garint out. Where does the jailer keep his keys?"

"On his belt I think. Why?"

Rouss frowned. "It will be difficult then." She glanced at her medicine bag in the corner. "I have an idea. Go back to Garint's house now. Stay there until this time tomorrow night."

He nodded, then hesitated as he picked up Garint's coat. He pecked her cheek. "Promise me you will consider what I have said."

Her eyes moistened as she studied his earnest face. "I will be unable to think of anything else. Now go." She opened the door and glanced out into the lane. "And stay out of sight of your friends in the red coats."

THE HERO

The swelling moon emerged from above the rooftops as Marin skulked down the lane to the cottage. Rouss flinched at the knock. She opened the door a crack. "Marin. You're early. Inside, quick." She opened the door wider and he stepped inside.

"I'm sorry. I couldn't wait." He looked at her black blouse, skirt, and coat topped by a long black cape. "You still wear the mourning clothes?"

She gave him a thin smile. "Tonight will be the last time." She turned to face the mirror on the wall beside the door and pulled the hood over her head. "Stay here until I get back." She nodded toward a neat stack on the bed. "Get changed into some of Leymo's clothes. I think those will fit you."

He nodded and stepped toward her. "Rouss."

She raised a gloved hand to stop him. "Please Marin, wait until I get back."

An hour later Marin paced the path behind Rouss's cottage. He watched his breath form icy clouds in the air in front of him.

Inside, Rouss buttoned up a green blouse which matched her eyes. The shimmering chinselk traced her curves from her shoulders to the belted waist of her flowing skirt. She fastened a silver chain around her neck and placed the cross carefully in a drawer. She hummed to herself to try to stop her mind from racing while brushing her hair in the mirror and chosing a colourful clasp to hold it in place. She bent down and opened a cupboard, searched in the back for an old bottle. Finding it, she drew it out and blew dust from it, frowned at the worm lying at the bottom. Top quality Meyco hooch, Leymo had said. His favourite. She removed the cork, filled two small glasses and placed them on the table, then went to the back door. "Marin," she whispered, "you can come in now."

Marin stepped back inside and draped his coat over a chair. His eyes widened as they took in her transformation. "You look more beautiful than ever."

She dropped her eyes and waved at the chair. "Please sit." Marin did as she bid and took a breath to speak before a loud knock interrupted him.

She put her finger to her lips. "Who is it?" she called.

"Rouss darra Sage, it's me, Bartim. I've come to talk with you again. I feel we parted unhappily last time we spoke and I would like to set things straight."

She looked at Marin. "It's late Mister Bartim. Perhaps tomorrow would be more appropriate?"

"I fear I have already left this too long. I have been thinking about the things you said."

"I am pleased to hear that Mister Bartim, but I don't feel this is the right time or place to continue that conversation." She looked at Marin and her face contorted in desperation.

Marin slid one hand inside his coat and pulled out a knife. Rouss glared at him and shook her head. The door latch scraped as Bartim tried the handle. Rouss spun around and lunged for the bolt but too late. The door opened and Bartim stepped in. He halted in mid stride. "Who is this?"

"An old friend." She took a breath. "Marin sunna Elevar, this is Eldmin and Mister Bartim." The men exchanged the barest of nods.

Bartim looked her up and down. "He is obviously someone worth dressing up for."

Rouss blushed. "He has brought me news of Leymo sunna Seena." She took a breath. "Marin has confirmed that he died at sea in a terrible storm."

Bartim nodded slowly and gestured to her clothes. "So, you are now ready to live again?"

"Yes." She flashed a glance at Marin.

"And you will accept my proposal?" He moved toward her.

"Not so fast." Marin stepped between them, the knife still clutched in one hand behind his back. "I have known Rouss for many years and loved her all that time. She is coming with me to the north."

Rouss raised her hands to separate them. "Sit down, both of you, and hear me out."

Marin and Bartim reluctantly lowered themselves into chairs on opposite sides of the table. Bartim picked up the glass, sniffed its contents, and downed it in one slug.

Rouss paced the room and wrung a handkerchief in her hands. "I have done a lot of thinking these past few days. About our discussion, Mister Bartim, the news of Leymo, Marin's return and escape . . ."

Bartim stared at Marin, his eyes ice cold. "You are the prisoner?"

Marin nodded, returning his glare. "It is not important. I will replace the glass."

Rouss ignored them and dabbed a tear with her handkerchief. "I have never felt more confused at any time in my entire life, but I think I am clear now."

She nodded to Marin. "One of you asks me to leave my home and venture into the wilderness and make a life somewhere I have never been."

She turned to Bartim. "The other allows me to stay in familiar surroundings, but I fear will require me to compromise too much. And that is not how I want to live, nor how I wish bring up a child, if Mam Gaia should bless me again."

Bartim scowled. Rouss blew her nose into the handkerchief.

"I have come to realise that I have other choices which I did not even consider before. My roots are here and my skills are still in demand, at least enough to keep bread on the table. Making babies is a growing concern in town these days." She attempted a smile. Neither Marin nor Bartim responded. The grin wilted on her lips. "I fear neither of you will like what I am about to say."

"What?" Marin pushed back his chair and leapt to his feet, hands clenched at his side. "You can't be thinking of accepting this oaf's proposal."

"You can curse me all you wish from your cell, deserter." Bartim rose, placed his hands on the table and leaned forward, glowering. "I will see you rot in jail."

"Stop it!" Rouss cried.

Knock, knock.

The rapping on the door froze them all. While time slowed to a glacial crawl, Rouss's mind raced. Had they found the sleeping jailer and the empty cell? Marin's face registered panic: had the Mounties discovered him? Bartim focussed on Marin, a glint of satisfaction flaring in his eyes, no doubt hoping it was the red jackets come to eliminate this new impediment to his plans.

Knock, knock.

Rouss turned her head toward the sound. Whatever lay outside it was too late. Fate would decide. "Come in," she croaked, barely able to get the words out.

The door opened and Garint limped inside, hair and beard brushed and wearing clean clothes. "I thought I'd get changed before I came over. Those Rosh clothes are . . ." His voice trailed off at the sight of Bartim and Marin.

Rouss smiled and rushed to embrace him. "Garint. Thank goodness you're safe."

———————

To learn more about the world of *Star's Reach*
and for links to purchase the novel and related works,
please visit intotheruins.com/stars-reach

WATER INK

BY RACHEL WHITE

When in seas deep and dark, only the gull flying high above knows where you swim.
— Mussip proverb

When in dark storm clouds, only fish in river currents far below know where you fly.
— another Mussip proverb

Jorna meandered downhill towards the riverbank, picking blueberries from bushes along the way. The late afternoon sun peeked through a few small gaps in the expanding cloud cover above her. The blueberries, wet from recent mist, glistened like jewels.

If it weren't for the sun's location, she would have lost track of time. She had left Klavoden in early morning, soon after she had finished helping her brother and mother clean the dishes and collect freshly laid eggs. Content with wherever her footsteps led her, Jorna had no destination that day. First she had ambled down towards the river valley and waded in the cool clear currents as minnows darted around her ankles. Returning back to shore, she peeled off some birch bark to make a miniature boat, adding a few twigs as passengers. After placing her boat in the water, she watched mesmerized as it swirled in eddies, eventually flowing downstream out of her view. She quietly told herself stories about the little people she imagined were in it, their adventures while flowing towards the ocean she had never seen. What other places would they pass by that she had never been? These stories petered out in her mind as her attention shifted to a spider spinning a web between two oak saplings. Later, when the sun was at its peak, she had found herself wandering towards the fields, following rabbit tracks with great intent until she became more interested in exploring the murky waters of Black Eye Pond nearby.

There she collected cattail leaves to make a basket, as black-and-white winged dragonflies flew in the air around her.

Today was not a particularly unusual day, as Jorna had spent many other days during her nine years of life exploring and playing in the forests and fields around Klavoden, often tagging along with Sarat or other village children. More recently, though, she wandered off alone. Drawn to solitude, Jorna had become a mystery in her village. Among people, she spoke very little, though she always listened attentively to stories others told. Lately, some villagers wondered what was on her mind. *What unique stories does she have yet doesn't share?* They tried to probe her with questions with little avail. Some villagers joked, "Squirrels and sparrows have likely heard Jorna's voice more than we have."

Arriving at the riverbank, she sat down on a rock, placed her half-filled basket on the ground beside her and rested, looking at the tan and reddish brown clay swirls below her feet. Her hands sank down, altering the patterns, and scooped up a clump with which she sculpted a girl who happened to look like Sarat—tall, long-haired, with a mischievous grin and an adventurous gaze. The clay figure evoked fond memories of times she and Sarat had spent together in the forest: Sarat teaching her how to skip stones on the river; the two of them catching bullfrogs and creating a song and dance about them; constructing stick shelters and making up stories about living in them; Sarat being bitten by a black snake she stepped on during a game of chase; making wildflower bouquets together to take back home; discovering a fawn sleeping on ferns . . .

Now Sarat was often elsewhere, learning of worlds to which Jorna was not yet privy. For a moment Jorna became aware of how alone she felt, despite the company of all the forest dwellers around her that usually made her feel welcome.

Perhaps because Sarat had entered her mind, Jorna picked up a stick, and despite not knowing how to correctly shape letters, she pretended to write in the clay. As she moved the stick back and forth through the red and brown surface, she imagined herself as a writer, scrawling a story that would be read by others far and wide. Elements of many stories told in the *Serclag* weaved into her story, yet the whole of it was her own.

The stick's movement in the clay soothed her, though no other person could have understood her made-up Mussip script. As water babbled continuously over stones, she felt as if the river at least understood the story she was so confidently imprinting into the clay:

> *Once upon a time a girl was born in a land lush with green grass, roaring rivers, and trees full of luscious fruits. Everyone in her village sang and spoke of their world's beauty and when she was very young she did too.*

One year a great drought ravaged the land and never ceased. The rivers shriveled up, the green grass grew brown, the fruit became dry, and the girl's voice dried up too into silence. Now the other villagers continued to be able to speak, but their voices changed. No one mentioned the drought or the world as it once was. Life continued; they ate dried fruits instead of juicy ones, and drank small drops of muddy water instead of jugs of crystal clear water. Some people grew hungry, others became sick, and every year some died but they were buried with no mention of the drought.

Whenever the girl would open her mouth as if to speak, never a sound would come out. No single human had ever heard her since she was young; they assumed she had nothing to say. One day she decided to run into a forest far away from any person, and to her surprise, she could speak. Deer, turtles, foxes, and grouses came and heard her. She was calm for a moment, but then she had to return to her village, and again no one could hear her voice. The next day the conversation around her grew too loud for her, so she ran again into the forest and spoke, and more animals gathered to listen.

At night she returned. All she could hear were crowds of people talking, but not one mentioned the drought. She tried again to speak but no sound came out. All she wished was to be rid of her misery of being mute in her village. She fell into a very deep sleep for many nights and days.

One day a large and loud party awakened her. Joyous cheers celebrated dried fields with nothing to harvest, people clanked wine glasses shallowly filled with murky water, and some enthusiastically danced to lively music about starving children. No one mentioned the drought that ravaged the land. Everyone seemed as merry as could be.

Exasperated, she ran off, this time not to the forest but to the driest of deserts where all was cracked earth and not a soul ventured. She knelt and wept deeply until all the tears within her had fallen out. She closed her eyes and wished she would soon die, but a sparrow suddenly landed on her shoulder and sweetly sang to her, "Open your eyes and look before you, little one." She looked at the puddle of tears that had now become a lake and saw herself reflected in its waters. Beneath her reflection, a voice was calling to her, "Dive in, dive in, my dear." She didn't know how to swim, *but she felt too paralyzed to do anything else, so she dove in. Finding she could swim, she ventured as deep as possible.*

At the bottom she discovered a small cottage and knocked on its door. An old woman invited her inside and fed her near the hearth. To her surprise she and the old woman talked for many hours. The girl told about all her miseries. Relieved, nourished, and understood, she wanted to stay there forever and never leave the cottage. But the old woman said "No," and shooed her out, but as she left, gave her a vessel from the hearth.

"Before leaving the lake, you must fill this up with water. When you return to your people, dip your hands in and speak. If you must, let your hands speak first by sprinkling water onto the world and then your voice will return . . ." And so the girl swam back to the surface . . .

Just as Jorna was about to finish her story, light rain interrupted her imagination, falling down on her and her story in river clay. Trying not to think about how her writing would soon be erased by the rain, she quickly dropped her stick, stood up, grabbed her basket, and ran up the trail towards Klavoden. She hastened, wanting to return home without getting drenched. Taking long but even strides, she tried to keep from spilling her basket of berries. Although the berries represented a small part of how she had spent the day, they somehow gave her confidence that her villagers would enthusiastically meet her and not ask too many questions about her explorations.

Within moments the light rain turned into a torrential downpour. There was no way she would arrive in Klavoden before becoming completely soaked. Accepting the futility of running, she slowed down and crouched below a hemlock to catch her breath and wait out the storm, though the branches weren't enough to keep her dry. She now accepted the heavy rain that only moments ago she had tried to outrun. Lightning flashed in the sky; thunder rumbled. Yet the rain calmed her, her anxiety dissolved and washed away. As water coated her skin, her longing for Sarat's company dissipated.

When it rained, she often thought of what Tyodor had told her. *Water is the ink that communicates the language of the world. It flows wordless stories. The stories we tell with words are echoes of water, but not the whole story. The beet, acorn, black walnut, and soot inks I make and write with are not substitutes for water, but with careful skill, can be a way to connect closer with it. My inks need water to work, yet the water in these inks do not give them their color. What is not water makes their form visible, yet their essence is not in the marks we see. No one is ready to become a writer without first understanding the language of water. So child, go forth far away from the inks we make and immerse yourself in forests and streams spun of water ink. Do not be afraid to get lost, for that is how you will find your way as a writer. Read and understand the stories it tells in the world all around and throughout us, even ones that will always be unknown. Even I remind myself and my fellow writers: When the dark ink forms drawn on pages have become more important and certain than the world around you, muting the voices of water, tear up those papers, return them to the soil, and learn to listen again to the forgotten language.*

It was evident to Jorna that Tyodor, despite being an author of nineteen books well known and revered by readers throughout Mussiplin, encouraged young villagers to learn the craft only when they were ready. She had run into him in the winter during *Lunoresli*—the full moon village feast. Despite her usual quietness, for the first time she had shared with him her desire to enter the *Beliodecan*—the writers' guild—and to learn the Mussip script.

"*Kayi len cribos dasya devin* . . . Why do you want to become a writer, Jorna?"

Jorna had shrugged. "*Na siya vhan* . . . I want to write down all my stories so others from far-away lands can read and know them. I want my stories to leave their footprints on paper and not disappear into darkness, so others can follow them. I long to discover secret worlds and stories I don't yet know by reading the papers that you and others have written." Then she added, "And I want to be like you and Sarat."

"Fair enough," Tyodor had responded. "But first I want to know you understand the language of the world in all its mystery, and know that every word you write can only hold a small part of its essence. Also, learn well the spoken stories, the ones told at the *Serclag* each week; let them reverberate in the waters deep within you, let them become a part of you as the air you breathe. The spoken ones are essential, for they arise from closer to the source, from the waters within us. They continually change as water flows; they don't linger long in one place as the written stories, yet their impermanence aids their survival. Then when you want to learn to write, you will learn how to make ink from berries, acorn, and soot; you will learn to grow flax and hemp from seed, collect milkweed, cattail, moss, and willow bark; your hands will get sticky making paper with these fibers; you will make pens from bamboo reeds or feathers. Maybe then you will be ready to learn how to shape letters and words onto paper. Merely learning word forms and willing them to appear, as if they are objects that stand alone outside the world, without knowledge of their source is not true writing. May I remind you: growing and harvesting fibers, making paper, ink, and pens are all part of the activity of written thought, just as much as moving the pen."

Jorna hadn't been surprised by how Tyodor had responded. For as long as she could remember, she had grown up knowing the value of *osyara*, the awareness of beginning to end, end to beginning of all of that flowed through her and others' lives. Whatever path a Mussip person took in life, it was only respected when approached with *osyara*. A cook had to deeply know where her *beva* grains, yams, *suclan* fruits, tomatoes and other food came from and had to participate in those cycles; if she did not, she was not a true cook. Similarly, an artist, to achieve any respect in Mussiplin, made her own paints and paper, knowing where they came from and where they might end up long after her death. A storyteller had to spend years learning not only from other storytellers but from the rhythms of water, to emulate qualities of water in her own telling. A storyteller mastered humility, knowing that the stories she told were once born and will die, giving life to other stories, all shadows of the wordless stories that permeate the world. A market trader had to demonstrate an intimate knowledge of the history of the products he exchanged, well beyond his immediate interaction with them, to become a trustworthy tradesperson. So it was not strange to Jorna that *osyara* was important for writers and readers too.

She knew that the worst insult in Klavoden was to be called a *yaegost*: one who defied *osyara*, who was blind to the flows that made one's life and activities possible, who refused to participate in those cycles. *Yaegosten* were scarce where she lived; she only remembered one time she witnessed someone seriously accused of being a *yaegost*. A craftsman had carved many beautiful bowls and had woven exquisite baskets. He brought them to market, yet he did not know the origins of the wood he used, having traded with a foreigner. One of Jorna's neighbors learned the wood came from a sacred grove of rare ash trees across the Hiyor River, now cut and stripped of most life. She remembered adults around her concluding that he was a *yaegost*. After much community discussion, he agreed to journey alone to the now mostly barren land and meditate among the tree stumps for several days, until *osyara* reemerged within himself.

Jorna was old enough to have heard stories about many other *yaegosten* though. She knew during one brief time long ago, there had been whole peoples of them who overran the world, devouring much of it. Because of their lack of *osyara*, they weren't stopped until the world had no more to give them. These *yaegosten* numbered many more than her people, but they did not survive long. *If we become yaegosten, we too will shrivel up*, her grandmother had reminded her more than once. Back in that time, Tyodor had told her, most writers didn't know how to make their own words; the forms were like amputated limbs of a tree, cut off from their life force, mutilated into tools that blinded people from *osyara*.

Jorna felt raindrops—colorless ink—pour down onto her skin, its stories resonating deep within her. She had envied Sarat who now had a key to a secret world, still foreign to Jorna. How she had recently longed to learn the kind of stories scrawled on flax and hemp paper, ones not heard in the *Serclag*. Sarat had been a friend for so long, but now it felt as though the worlds they inhabited were growing apart. *When can I attain the power that Sarat is gaining?*

For those moments though, the drops of water soothed her. She felt the clouds the water had fallen from, the streams it had flowed in, the deer and squirrels who had drunk it. The rain was drops from melting snows, ocean currents far away, trees growing, the blood in her body, the moist afternoon air, her sweat before it had been rinsed off by rain, all her ancestors, and children yet to be born—weaving all of life together. She still looked forward to one day entering the *Beliodecan*, but she hoped she would never lose this feeling of belonging, which was greater than any language she would write. She felt a power she could never steal for herself, for she was a part of it.

Jorna and her brother sat down on a hand-woven mat in the *Serclag*. The last remains of sunlight faded into darkness and the north wind blew in through the four passageways, gently caressing the villagers who had gathered. She couldn't count how many times she had come here for stories, nor remember when had been the first time. Probably she had first come within days after emerging from her mother's womb, long before she could understand the meaning of all the story words. She imagined herself here as a newborn baby in her mother's arms, hearing a flow of inseparable sounds from the storyteller's mouth. Maybe the storyteller's voice had felt like the rhythm of water to Jorna's ears: a waterfall pouring down . . . into stream . . . becoming stagnant pond . . . its surface freezing . . . ice dripping . . . puddles forming . . . evaporating into air . . . forming clouds . . . sprinkles falling . . . becoming showers . . . ending in silent calm. Now she could understand the words. But the words still felt like water; stories she heard again and again entered into her anew each time, for her reflection she saw in them each time changed. The story was always more than the words; it could not survive without flowing throughout its people, the landscape, the present moment.

A circular fence made of willow sticks, its height shorter than a young child, outlined the *Serclag*, the village center. There was no ceiling but the starry or cloudy sky, except on rainy evenings, when villagers attached a cloth from the high poles at each passageway. Several storytellers regularly took turns leading the evenings, though most villagers had told a story here on occasion. Tonight Norenay had entered the center ring, waiting for all the villagers to find their place.

The *Serclag* centered Jorna's life as it did her village. As she sat quietly, many stories she had breathed in at the *Serclag*, that had woven her life and world together into a whole, wandered through her mind: *The Days the Flowers Had No Bees*

. . . When Willow Branches Reached Towards the Stars and Began to Weep . . . The Owl Who Found His Voice in Darkness . . . The Boy Who Tried to Steal Water . . . Fawwa, The Man Who Wanted to Live Forever . . . The Fish Who Thought She Had No Home . . .

What story would Norenay tell tonight? she wondered.

More stories she had heard during the past nine years flooded into awareness: *The Yaegost Who Drew Time . . . The Water Strider and His Reflection . . . The Living Dead Who Failed to Kill Death . . . A Story That Disappeared With the Fog . . . Parahi, the Crying Girl Who Caught Laughter . . . The Black Soup That Tried to Replace Water . . .*

Villagers' voices around her quieted down as Norenay slowly danced one time around the center, spreading her arms out invitingly towards every villager, signaling she was about to begin.

"Heth begunt lama nin linguna pint reyi beba ben shunt del casanta . . ." Norenay began, pretending to cradle a baby with her arms, as she spoke Mussip in her Harpten accent, having grown up in the nearby village. "In the beginning, the ancestors of people were like a baby, born with no words. The trees, the soils, the rain, the clouds, the deer, the stones existed, but they were known by their texture, smells, sounds, and colors, as an inseparable, unnamed world, as a baby first knows it. The first people discovered different utterances they could make, and they began to name the world. Trees got names, stones got names. So did the waters, the sun, moon, and stars, the wind, the mountains, the animals they hunted, and the fruits they gathered. And the people named each other.

"Their naming gave them power. It helped them find food, survive both the cold and heat, raise children, learn to make fire, and later plant crops. They told stories, just like I tell stories to you, passed down to children, then to their children's children. Some people also began to paint the world into new shapes with colors from stones, clay, and berries. But their words and stories and pictures intermingled with the waters and soil, unable to be plucked apart, for the sounds and images came from within and could not survive long on their own in open air."

Norenay brought her hands to her chest, then outward, more and more softly as they traveled further from her, as if they were evaporating into the air. Jorna intently listened, recognizing the story, but still mesmerized by Norenay's current telling.

"Many, many years passed, and then something changed. Why it changed is a story . . . or many stories . . . for another time. Some people allowed words to escape from their mouths and rise up and linger in the air as if they were their own beings. A word did not just begin and end; the beginning and end could be seen at the same time, staying much longer after they were uttered. Even though human hands had created their ancestors, these words were like animals with heads, tails, and legs enabling them to run far on their own.

"As these words ran throughout the world, they started to cast their shadows all around, their outlines rapidly multiplying onto the landscape. Human hands that had once birthed and molded the distant ancestors of these shadows became hidden from sight. Many people rejoiced in this new power, for their words could travel very quickly far and wide, and to many places at once. A few people reached into the air to pull the detached words back to the world womb where they had once emerged, but their arms were too small and too few to slow the thick clouds forming. Several people tried to attach leashes to words to keep them close to earth; but others tore those away. Many people eagerly jumped onto these words, asserting their independence from the world. They floated far away, as if they would soon reach the stars.

"Words cast more shadows into the air, and those shadows cast more shadows, and those even more shadows, and yet more shadows, until a fog covered much of the world's surface. Then pictures grew out of some of these word-shadows, not pictures like the ones we paint on earth, but ones whose fiber threads were cut off from the world, dancing around as if they were all-powerful beings without a creator. The pictures that appeared in each generation became more exquisite and real-looking than the ones before. For a few moments many pictures could move and talk in the air on their own; some could skillfully pretend to engage people as if they were the world itself. Oh, even if their underside was ugly and they were deceiving, the surfaces of many pictures were majestic, brilliantly colorful, entrancing, much more than any of our Mussip sketches on *fouza* rolls. These pictures became people's houses and villages; they lived in them day and night, for they believed these pictures were sturdier and more trustworthy than any home they knew before.

"When people saw a majestic castle on the horizon, in swirls of fog, housing all the dreams and sweetness and comfort they desired, they believed it. Even during a brief clearing, when an honest child pointed out there was no castle there, but ruins rusting and rotting in the ground and a poisoned pond, they ridiculed the child, for the fog picture was trusted more than the world beyond. The people were thirsty for what they believed they saw on the surface; they kept seeking more of the fog-world but it only made them thirstier. The real waters that would have quenched their thirst were invisible to them. The original source of the fog's pictures remained more and more hidden to the people, like an occasional pesky vine that crept through their house walls that they usually ignored. The pictures became the world, and the world a pest to be squelched.

"The fog grew denser and denser; the words and pictures grew like algae in a pond, a seemingly unstoppable force that no one could contain. For a brief time the words and pictures reached a zenith of power. The fog blocked the view of forests, mountains, and streams. So dense was the fog that many forgot the world they no longer saw and mistook the fog, all arisen from people, as the world itself. Even when they believed they had power, people were desperately lost, for the clarity of streams and springs were out of reach. Brawls broke out among people. Words fought words. Pictures fought other pictures. Much blood and poison spread throughout the fog-world.

"As the fog-world became uglier, the soils and streams unseen began to dry up and become poisoned. The fog had rejected its mother, asserting it had no use for her. 'Trust me more than the soils and streams,' it demanded. 'I am immortal, clean, all dirt fallen away; worship me as Truth.'

"People, even those growing unhappy and gasping for air in fog, thought their world of words and pictures, seeming to possess great power, would grow and grow forever. But a few perceptive people who lived in a fog clearing—Tuvenora and her brother Garen—noticed that large pools of black sticky ink were being sucked dry to keep the fog-world alive. The fog-world tapped into the veins of these black pools, which powered the grandeur of its words and pictures, most of which en-couraged even more sucking up of black ink. A dangerous cycle! When they told what they saw, others ridiculed them. The fog-world denied its need of black pools. When Tuvenora shone a light on the black veins becoming fog, the fog-world in-sisted there were endless pools and not to worry for the creativity of its pictures en-sured forever abundance. 'Never worry, for I am an all-powerful world; everything else obeys me,' it seemed to shout.

"'We need to rescue the words and pictures!' cried Tuvenora. 'They are devour-ing the world, fooling the people. They are not the world; they cannot live forever on their own. One day when the black pools completely dry out, both they and much of the world beyond will be gone. The world will be again speechless, barren in plain sight, poorer than before, all that had once nourished us scraped away.'

"'All the better,' her brother Garen replied. 'There's no use for any words and pictures of the fog-world. All deserve to die along with us. All they do is destroy. The words deserve to meet their end as no more than shattered smithereens, never to exist further. Let us return to the speechless, picture-less world and not risk this again. The entire journey was a mistake.'

"'No!' Tuvenora angrily responded. 'It is the fog-world that makes us think there are only two choices to tragedy. Let us not let our minds become tainted with fog too in this moment; let us be open to other options. Let us pay attention to the latent images within us, long suppressed by the fog. They emerge for a reason and may give us direction. What if we weave words back into the world, so they no longer float alone and detached in the air? All power is not bad. The power must not be at odds with the world or it becomes weakness. Our power must come home now, for it comes from the world, not us.'"

As Jorna intently listened to Norenay's voice, she looked up at a wood carving of Tuvenora standing beside one of the *Serclag* passageways. The Mussip people believed that Tuvenora and her family were their ancestors, responsible for all the words and stories on which their lives depended. Jorna felt as if Tuvenora was present there in the *Serclag*, dancing among the words coming out of Norenay's mouth.

"Moments before all the clouds of words started to shrivel up, when the black pools were almost depleted, Tuvenora weaved a net out of willow limbs. She reached it up into the air, rescued a few of the important words, especially those struggling to find a way back to earth. Those words fluttered like butterflies, unaware where the journey was taking them, and were brought back home just before they would have shriveled up with the rest.

"Most of the pictures were so big, tangled with each other in endless knots and dependent on disappearing black ink, that they were impossible to catch and save in Tuvenora's net. These pictures, along with the rest of the words, insisted on their eternity to their end, as they flashed one last brilliant outburst before shriveling into darkness, suffering a magnificent death. Without these pictures, many people who had lived within them despaired, felt lost, and died too, for these pictures had housed their souls. They knew of no other life.

"Tuvenora introduced words again to the soils, the currents of streams and oceans, embedded them in clay, and weaved them into stories that the fish, bees, and flowers liked. These stories intertwined with the world, becoming an inseparable tapestry. Those people who did not die with the pictures learned to give birth to their own images again, too long repressed, with colors and patterns that nestled well into the landscape.

"... And our stories, like the one I just told you, live on because of Tuvenora. She saved the essential words, and spread the ashes of many dead ones onto the soil to nourish the great growth of new ones that would stay rooted in earth."

Norenay's hands rose up to her mouth, then gestured outward, as if she was holding many word-strands, weaving them into the circle of villagers and the world beyond. As her hands swayed in the cool evening air, she began to softly hum, gradually louder as she invoked Tuvenora's presence, "*La eth, sa ma Tuvenora ra dyen. Tuvenora, Tuvenora, Tuvenora . . . shay meya locan. . . . Tuvenora. . . .*"

Jorna, along with the other Klavoden villagers, rose up, humming too. Then, as always after a story, they joined together in song, and began to dance in a spiral pattern, the outside line of villagers weaving in and out of the *Serclag*, as if the center and its surroundings were becoming one tapestry.

"*Jay agnan dun vench nutris . . .*" Jorna radiantly began to sing, as she imagined the words being saved by Tuvenora's net, and others sprouting from ashes of those that died, becoming part of the Klavoden houses, fields and forests beyond. Her body knew these songs and dances as effortlessly as she breathed:

From waters deep we came
We rose up to breathe the endless air

In clear skies above
We saw the seas below

Storm clouds darkened our eyes
Lightning splintered us

As raindrops we return
With a little sky
To the waters of our womb

And emerge anew.

‡‡

Far beyond the rolling meadows Jorna could faintly see it. The stone and cob building stood at the edge of the distant forest, a small yet important structure growing larger in her view. That morning she had left Klavoden, hiked past the villages of Juran, Harpten, and Moneck, through familiar forests and fields, hopped on rocks across streams, climbed over hills, all on the same path she walked on now. The midday sun shone brightly above her, her body exhausted from its heat. Yet she eagerly skipped onward. Soon she would discover the new world Sarat had entered.

After the last *Lunoresli*, Tyodor had found Jorna alone with a twig, scribbling designs only she understood onto the sand, whispering to herself one of her many made-up stories.

Tyodor observed, "There's a writer within you ready to come into being."

"Oh, how I wish I could write Mussip like you so that others could read my words!" Jorna exclaimed longingly.

"Jorna, for nine years you have immersed yourself in forests and streams. You've listened to the language of rivers and stones, skies and soil as it flows into you. This language is a part of you; now it flows out of you through your unique voice, yearning to travel far into the world. I now trust you will uphold *osyara* as you gain new abilities in *Beliodecan*. We welcome you to join us following the next new moon."

Tyodor's recent words glowed radiantly inside her, as if a ray of the bright sun above had entered within her.

Jorna knew it would disrupt *osyara* for children to be quickly rushed to the

Beliodecan at an early age; they came when they were ready. A few at five or six, some at seven or eight, some like her at nine, some even later. . . . Until recently Jorna had never contemplated the manner in which children came to the *Beliodecan*. It seemed as it has always been, in the same way it was obvious that a *Serclag* must center every village, or that children should spend many days playing in the forest away from adults, or that all people knew the movements of stars in the sky. But Sarat had mentioned that she explored several large rooms in the *Beliodecan*. Mussip books, made of hemp, willow, cattail, or flax, filled most of these rooms. However, some ancient books, including some *yaegost* ones, occupied one room. A few of those carefully preserved books, their pages covered with foreign script and bright pictures, had been made for very young children—yet they were only simple samples of many more manufactured worlds that had existed, yet more elaborate with sounds and bright moving colors, though none of those survived. That seemed so strange to Jorna! Sarat explained that *yaegosten* immersed their children in a thick fog of *yaegost* words and pictures and stories at birth, rushing them away from both the world beyond and within them, so they would grow up to be *yaegosten*. Did *yaegost* children ever learn the language of forests and rivers and skies? Very rarely, Sarat had replied. *Yaegosten* valued skills that helped them live in the fog-world, for that was the only world many knew.

As Jorna contemplated this peculiarity of a brief distant time, the *Beliodecan* grew larger and larger into view, until there it stood in front of her on a small hill on the other side of a bridge. Jorna walked confidently across the bridge, her ears filled with sounds of water babbling over stones. That water had flowed past the river clay where she had scrawled made-up word forms days before. She could feel her life thus far flowing towards what she would soon learn. Happily she told herself the ending of her story that began in the river clay, imagining she'd be able to write it in the days ahead:

> *. . . and before the girl left the lake, she scooped the vessel into the water and filled it to the brim, then hurried back to the lands of her village. She sprinkled water in beautiful designs on the dry grass and shriveled fruit trees and the thirsty, talkative people. The green grass grew, the fruit became juicy, and rivers reformed in the crevices of the land. People's voices changed, as they suddenly spoke of the drought that had ended. There was one last drop of water left, which she swallowed, and her voice was restored. From then on her villagers heard her words. They decided to put the vessel into the earth where it became the village Well of Wisdom and for the rest of her life the girl gathered stories there to nourish the villagers.*

Maybe writing would feel like bringing water from within and sprinkling it in intricate designs onto dry areas where speech suffered, giving voice to once barren lands, and reviving her own voice. She looked forward to writing down the many stories she had quietly told herself, yet to be known by anyone else.

Her gaze moved forward. A deep and dense pine forest gradually merged into the right side of the main *Beliodecan* building structure, for she could not see the exact line where the walls ended and the forest began. Sarat had told her she and other writers would amble throughout the pines to write and read; the forest was considered part of the *Beliodecan* as much as the building center. Surrounding the building's left side, fields of flax and hemp grew. Jorna could also see the green, yellow, purple and red of vegetables, fruit trees, and berries growing in a garden near a side entrance. The building's walls curved with the contours of the land. The stone structure looked strong and older than her village's houses, yet aired a humble presence within the land. Staring at the scene in front of her, she tried to imagine new worlds she would discover inside and outside, what writers she would meet on pages and in person. What would the first few months be like for her, making paper and ink, then learning to form them into Mussip words on pages? One day, like Sarat, she would easily read books . . .

Jorna arrived at the oak door entrance. Before knocking, she glanced above and noticed an engraved drawing on stone. The etched image, partially moss-covered, looked ancient, its outlines faint to her eyes. But that only drew her to look at it more closely. There she saw Tuvenora kneeling on the ground, beside a stream. In the left corner above Tuvenora were fragments of unknown objects that dissipated as they moved across the picture, like an explosion becoming nothingness. Tuvenora's hands spread out, holding some Mussip script, unintelligible to Jorna. She was weaving the word threads into the landscape, creating a tapestry.

Completely absorbed, Jorna stared for a while at the image. In those moments, she felt profoundly Tuvenora's presence. Jorna felt like her own life story would nestle within Tuvenora's, along with all the stories she had heard at the *Serclag*, her many made-up tales including the one about her birch bark passengers and the one she had scrawled in river clay, the wordless stories she felt in the forest, and new ones she had yet to learn here. All these stories were like overlapping layers of sycamore bark, forming one whole trunk of life. At different places different shades of bark appeared, yet they were inseparable from the rest.

Tyodor opened the door, interrupting her thoughts. "*Bayan hideros* . . . Welcome, Jorna! So glad you have finally arrived." He paused, waiting to hear a response from Jorna, but she remained quiet.

"You look like you've had a long journey. I will get you a glass of water, let you rest a bit, then show you around and discuss your first few days here. By the way,

Sarat is very excited to see you, but you will have to wait a little bit, because right now she's out collecting some willow bark."

Jorna shyly nodded, her gaze still directed towards the moss-covered etching above.

"I see you notice the stone carving above—you look like you are meditating on it, although you can't yet read it. We writers and readers reflect too on it daily, for it helps focus our work. How about I read it to you?"

Jorna's eyes silently answered yes.

Tyodor looked above the oak door, and with a voice as rhythmically flowing as the waters she had just passed over, read the rescued words Tuvenora was weaving into the world:

May our words be a way to go beyond them.
May they dissolve boundaries that they create.
May we understand their importance through their unimportance.
May their weaknesses be their strength.
May we find freedom in their limits.
May we know them so well that they become a mystery.
May their taming lead us to wildness.
May what stays the same with them allow them to change.
May their death give birth to them.
May our words flow like water but never be water.

Tyodor pulled the door handle, and Jorna, thirsty for water, entered inside.

REVIEWS

TWO FROM THE FAR FUTURE

The Winter of the World
by Poul Anderson

New American Library, 1975

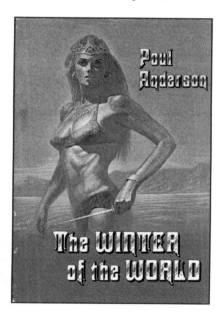

&

The Pastel City
by M. John Harrison

Avon Books, 1971

ONE OF THE OPPORTUNITIES science fiction offers writers and readers alike is the chance to step outside the narrow confines of the present day, and view the human prospect from some less parochial perspective than the one defined for each of us by the time, the place, and the culture in which we happen to be born. That opportunity isn't always taken up; as every reader of science fiction knows, there are too many tales supposedly set on distant planets in the far future that remain firmly stuck in familiar ruts once you look past the freshly painted scenery.

Turn the pages of Isaac Asimov's *Foundation Trilogy*, to cite just one example, and you can count on being bowled over, not by strangeness, but by embarrassing familiarity. Even though the story's supposedly set so far in the future that nobody remembers that humanity originated on Earth, the characters think, talk, and act like middle-class Americans from the 1950s. Their technology and social forms copy that model so rigidly that the reader is left wondering why *Leave It To Beaver* isn't playing on the telescreens.

Fortunately, there are also plenty of

science fiction stories that manage to dodge that trap, and some very good examples are found in deindustrial science fiction. To some extent, that's hardwired into the nature of the deindustrial subgenre; pretty much by definition, if you're writing a story set in a future following the decline and fall of modern industrial civilization, your setting is going to evoke a sharp contrast between today's world and the very different world of the future you're describing in your fiction.

Even so, the contrast can be handled in many ways, and to my mind, one of the most striking is the perspective of deep time—the sort of view from afar that's offered by a story set not decades or centuries after industrial civilization, but tens of millennia or more. Each of the two novels up for discussion in this issue's column achieves that perspective, showing the reader a little of what our time looks like from the perspective of the very far future—and in each novel, those glimpses are understated details scattered here and there in a lively tale.

Poul Anderson's *The Winter of the World* doesn't get much discussion in mainstream SF these days, because it was written at a time when some reputable climate scientists believed that a new ice age was on the way, and it's become inconvenient for climate scientists today to admit that this ever happened. *The Winter of the World* is set squarely in that imagined ice age future, some tens of thousands of years from now, when sea levels are hundreds of feet lower than they are today, climate belts have shifted dramatically, and vast ice sheets sprawl over much of the world, covering the northern half of the continent that we call North America and the people of that time call Andalin.

Two great powers contend for dominance in that future world. The great maritime commonwealth of Killimaraich, from its homeland in eastern Orenstane (that's pronounced "Australia" these days), dominates much of the world's navigable oceans, and pursues science and technology within the hard limits of a planet with very little iron or fossil fuels. The empire of Rahid, rooted in what we would call the northern half of Mexico and the southwest United States, was conquered a few generations back by highland clans from Baromm further south—those of my readers who've read anything about the Mongol or Manchu conquests of China already know the same tune in a different key—and the united Rahidian-Barommian Empire has set its sights on world dominion. Between them lies the fantastically ancient metropolis of Arvanneth, located not far inland from the mouth of the Jugular River (we'd say "Mississippi"), which has recently fallen to the Empire's Army of the North under its brilliant Captain-General Sidír; filter the name of the city through tens of thousands of years of multilingual mumbling and you just might hear its ancient name New Orleans. North of Arvanneth, finally, lies the prairie and tundra realm of the enigmatic Rogaviki, seminomadic hunter-folk whose lands are the Empire's next target.

To Arvanneth comes Josserek Derrain, secret agent of Killimaraich, to make contact with the resistance movement within Arvanneth and, through them, the Rogaviki. The events that follow—and I'm not going to risk spoiling a tale this good by saying too much about those—entangle Derrain, the Barommian commander Sidír, and the Rogaviki not-quite-leader Donya of Hervar in each other's lives and destinies, as Sidír leads the Army of the North to the edge of the Ice and the ruins of Unknown Roong, and Derrain and Donya rally the Rogaviki and the people of Arvanneth to stop the Empire's march of conquest. It's a grand story—and then there's Anderson's prose, which is lean, elegant, and utterly suited to the story. Here's the beginning of the novel, as perfect an evocation of place and time as you'll find anywhere:

"Once during the Ice Age, three men came riding to Owlhaunt, where Donya of Hervar had her wintergarth. This was on the Stallion River, northwest of the outpost Fuld by four days' travel which the wayfarer from Arvanneth found hard. The sun had entered the Elk last month and now was aloft longer than a night lasted. Nevertheless, earth still was white; the old stiff snow creaked beneath hooves. A wind, cutting across level evening light, carried a feel of tundras beyond the horizon and glacial cliffs beyond those."

In the tapestry of war, love, and the clash of civilizations that Anderson un-

folds, our civilization is a dim background presence at most. The scholars of Killimaraich are pretty sure that the great ice sheets haven't been there forever, and that there was an ancient civilization before the Ice came; scattered ruins and relics here and there hint at the shape of that forgotten society; and then there are curious geological features in certain parts of the world that look like great bowls or kettles scooped out by unimaginable forces in the distant past, and excavation into them reveals layers of rock fused by great heat. How they got there, nobody knows, but it might have happened around the beginning of the Ice Age.

The fact that the only petroleum deposits anyone can find in this distant future are in areas that were deep underwater in ancient times is one more piece of the puzzle. Then there's Unknown Roong, a city on the edge of the ice sheets, mined for metal by the Rogaviki but otherwise largely untouched, like abandoned huts in the Antarctic today, due to the terrible cold. The journey of Sidír and his soldiers to Roong is among the high points of the story, a harrowing confrontation with time and the limits of human existence.

Anderson handles all this with his trademark skill. The technology and weaponry of his far future civilizations are carefully thought out; windmills and solar water heaters are present, and steam engines are a known technology, but expensive to fuel and so uncommon; firearms are more metal-intensive than edged weapons, and so the armies of the Rahidian-Barommian Empire resemble seventeenth-century European armies, with lancers on horseback, infantry equipped with swords and spears, and riflemen providing the same sort of support that musketeers did in the English Civil War and the Thirty Years War. Neither Killimaraich nor Rahid nor Arvanneth nor the Rogaviki are a modern industrial civilization like ours, nor will they ever be: a matter of a few tens of thousands of years, vast though that is from the human perspective, isn't enough to begin replenishing the energy and mineral resources we waste so carelessly.

At the same time, the peoples of Anderson's future ice age aren't simply reflections of some corner of our past. They offer a potent reminder that human history isn't a straight line leading to us, and when it scrolls out beyond us into the distant future, it may head in directions we can't imagine today. *The Winter of the World* thus counts as a significant work of deindustrial SF, and deserves more than one reading.

The Pastel City by M. John Harrison gets to the same place by nearly the opposite route. Harrison's tale is basically a sword-and-sorcery epic, except that the place of sorcery is occupied by the fragmentary but functional technologies of a long-dead civilization—and no, this wasn't ours. "Some seventeen notable empires," Harrison tells us, "rose in the Middle Period of Earth.

These were the Afternoon Cultures. All but one are unimportant to this narrative, and there is little need to speak of them save to say that none of them lasted for less than a millennium, none for more than ten; that each extracted such secrets and obtained such comforts as its nature (and the nature of the Universe) enabled it to find; and that each fell back from the Universe in confusion, dwindled, and died."

It's a stunningly effective way of creating imaginative distance. Even if modern industrial civilization counts as the first of the Afternoon Cultures, and for all the reader ever finds out, it might be one of the last of the utterly forgotten Morning Cultures instead, a gap that can't be measured in mere millennia opens up between us and the people of Viriconium, the first of the Evening Cultures. We are further from them, and thus matter less to them, than the civilization of ancient Sumer was and mattered to the people of the dark age civilizations that rose in Europe after the fall of Rome. The civilization that matters in Viriconium's day was the last of the Afternoon Cultures, which left behind technologies that still remain lethally viable a thousand years after their makers passed through the familiar arc of decline and fall.

Given that degree of distance, managing enough familiarity to make a story appealing to readers back here in the forgotten past is a challenging trick, but Harrison manages it by a device that's at once commonplace and profoundly insightful. It so happens that when civilizations fall, the sort of societies that emerge out of the ensuing dark ages all follow the same general pattern, even when the civilizations that fell were sharply different. Mycenean Greece, Heian Japan, and the Roman Empire didn't have much in common, for example, but the hardscrabble societies that emerged out of them—pre-classical Greece, the Japan of the Kamakura and Muromachi periods, and early medieval Europe—were astonishingly similar, with quarrelsome feudal aristocracies, warrior castes on horseback, and epic poetry as the principal literary form. The similarities are astonishing—between the medieval European code of chivalry and the medieval Japanese code of bushido, for example, the differences have to be measured with a micrometer.

The same is true, in Harrison's vision, even after the rise and fall of the Afternoon Cultures. Viriconium is a standard late dark age society on the brink of its own post-Afternoon middle ages, in the midst of a revival of learning and culture brought about by the long reign of a successful warrior king—those of my readers who've read anything about Charlemagne or Alfred the Great, again, already know the same tune in a different key. In Viriconium, the warrior king was Methven Nian, and the enemies against which he and his inner circle of warriors battled were still-barbarian tribes dwelling in the bleak, ruin-dotted wastelands of the north. The story opens ten years after Methven's death; his daughter Methvel reigns in Viriconium; Methven's warrior elite has scattered; and in time, the north rises again.

The central character of the tale, tegeus-Cromis, is one of Methven's veteran warriors, lean and cadaverous, the deadliest swordsman in the realm. As renewed war breaks out, he travels to Viriconium to offer his services to the queen, and then proceeds to the front, only to witness catastrophic defeat. The northern tribes have unearthed a ghastly technology from the distant past and unloosed it on Viriconium, heedless of the long-term consequences. The survival of humanity is at stake as tegeus-Cromis and a small band of friends—the brawling blond warrior Birkin Grif; Tomb the Dwarf, skilled at salvaged technologies; and Queen Methvet herself, driven from her throne by the northern tribes—ride into the wasteland to find a forgotten site where, just possibly, the menace of the *geteit chemosit*, "the eaters of brains," can be ended.

As already noted, it's a sword-and-sorcery tale with the sorcery provided by Afternoon Culture technology. In place of magical swords and the like are *baans*, energy blades kept in ceramic sheaths, which can slice through flesh and bone like butter. (*The Pastel City* was published well before *Star Wars* premiered so, no, *baans* aren't second-hand light sabers; if anything, the influence may have gone the other way.) The nearest thing to a wizard in the story, the mysterious being named Celuur, has "familiars" in the form of metallic robot birds; again, technology takes the place of sorcery. The *geteit chemosit*, whose fantasy equivalents would fall somewhere on the spectrum between orcs and demons, have that peculiar mindless malevolence that industrial technology so often achieves even in our time.

In less competent hands the replacement of magic by advanced technology might have seemed clumsy or unconvincing, but Harrison pulls it off with aplomb. His prose style, like that deployed by Poul Anderson, is an important part of his success. Here's the beginning of the first chapter, as neat an evocation as the opening sentences of *The Winter of the World*, though here what's being evoked is character and context rather than place and time:

"tegeus-Cromis, sometime soldier and sophisticate of Viriconium, the Pastel City, who now dwelt quite alone in a tower by the sea and imagined himself a better poet than swordsman, stood at early morning on the sand-dunes that lay between his tall home and the grey line of the surf. Like swift and tattered scraps of rag, black gulls sped and fought over his downcast head. It was a catastrophe that had driven him from his tower, something that he had witnessed from its topmost room during the night."

Another crucial element of Harrison's success, though, is the way that the landscape through which tegeus-Cromis journeys is as thoroughly marked by ancient technology as your average fantasy novel landscape is by ancient magic. There are deserts of rust, the remnants of ancient industrial hinterlands; there's the Metal-salt Marsh, poisoned by runoff from the wastelands; there is the half-drowned city known only as Thing Fifty; there's Viriconium itself, the remnant of a city of the last Afternoon Culture patched up with timber and stonework: in such a setting, the energy blades and robot birds and *geteit chemosit* fit as comfortably and naturally as magic swords and fire-breathing dragons fit in the settings of more ordinary fantasy. It's a bravura performance, and well worth the attention of writers and readers of deindustrial SF today.

———————

In future issues of *Into the Ruins*, I plan on continuing this column and surveying the desolate but enticing landscapes portrayed by past authors of deindustrial SF. While I have a good many books already lined up to review, there's doubtless no shortage of stories of that kind that I haven't read or don't remember. If you have favorites you'd like to propose for review, or for that matter really dreadful examples of the species, by all means drop me a note c/o *Into the Ruins* at joel@intotheruins.com, or by mail at:

Figuration Press
3515 SE Clinton Street
Portland, OR 97202

Many thanks!

THE CITIZENS OF UNION GROVE

BY JUSTIN PATRICK MOORE

MY COPY OF *THE HARROWS OF SPRING* by James Howard Kunstler arrived in the mail on a day that turned out to be auspicious. As the final volume in a four part series that began in 2008 with *World Made By Hand*, I had eagerly awaited each new book in this seasonal cycle portraying the intertwined lives of the citizens of Union Grove, a fictional town set on the banks of the Battenkill river north of Albany in New York. Off work that afternoon, I delved into the early chapters before taking a lazy summer nap with my beloved wife. As we dozed, a strange sound woke us up, followed by a flicker of electricity, a sudden quiet, and then voices on the street.

The old hollow silver maple tree in my neighbor's yard had fallen from a gust of wind as a nearby thunder storm pounded adjacent neighborhoods with thick spools of rain. The tree had fallen into the power lines and knocked off the chimney of the Hispanic church on the corner of the street. Just after the tree fell, my step-daughter dropped off our grand-son to watch for the night. Soon I found myself chopping vegetables in the candlelight, preparing dinner on our 1940s era gas stove while Audrey read Lucas a story. My rotary phone land line was still getting its low voltage signal, and I had battery power for my ham radio upstairs if I needed to communicate before the power company got the juice flowing again. I thought of the weather, and how strange and frequent the storms are getting here in the Ohio valley. As I cut carrots and kale for our impromptu soup, I also reflected on the town of Union Grove. I had become quite attached to the goings on in that town where the electricity had been off for much longer than an evening, where there were no utility companies around anymore. No cheap source of power to keep the darkness at bay. No quick flick of a switch to keep folks locked into the illusion that they are separate from nature.

In the background of this series, a number of smaller and larger catastrophic events lead up to the disheveled stage where characters take actions, and where actions forge character. Encephalitis and various strains of flu had culled large swathes of the human population. Washington D.C. was bombed. The wheels of government from local to federal had disappeared altogether for the most part. Oil had run out and shipments of mass produced goods faltered and stopped. People have new choices to make, and plenty of things that need to be done by the sweat of their own labor, the work of their own hands. Some go the way of everyday cowards and others everyday heroes. Some just grit their teeth and get on with things through sheer determination. If a person's basic character has a guiding influence over their actions inside an ecology of limits, than the study of fictional characters can be a form of guidance and inspiration. It shows the readers of deindustrial SF the broad contours and possibilities of the future and can help them shape their own destiny in an optimistic way. No matter the cut of their cloth, the citizens of Union Grove and its outlying counties have a lot to teach in Kunstler's rendition of the not-distant future.

The events of *World Made By Hand*, the first volume of the four, take place over a summer whose long days are filled with a broad array of activities. For Robert Earle, a former software executive turned carpenter, it means fishing with his friend Loren who is minister of the town church, sawing and nailing on different jobs around town and trying not to worry about the fate of his son Daniel who left town two years before to see what had become of the rest of America. Robert has so much work on his hands he has much more to do than he has time to think about, and this helps him keep the demons of fret and worry at bay. As a widower whose wife died in an epidemic, Robert could have been complacent. Instead he chose to apply himself in the face of hardship. He brought out his dormant woodworking skill set and started doing what was needed. In time he becomes a stalwart member of town, and eventually its mayor. The warp and weft of the books wraps around this man. As the strange and tragic events of these stories unfolded, I was privileged to see him in the full range of his humanity—shaken by loss, grief and fear but always moving beyond it to take action on the matters that spoke to his soul.

The arrival of Brother Jobe and his pious flock of seventy-three adults also occurs in the first volume. As the shepherd of a group of newfangled evangelical Christians fleeing from civil unrest and hardships in Virginia he has the kind of guile and charisma that is sometimes expected out of a Southern preacher—or lawyer, as he was in the old times before he turned his life over to the Lord. Gifted with the skills of mind reading and hypnotism, Kunstler uses Brother Jobe as one of his ploys for reintroducing the dimension of the ineffable, of the supernatural and sacred, into the arc of the overall story of Union Grove. As the promises of modernity fall apart they are in many cases replaced with spiritual and religious inclinations. And while belonging to a Judeo-Christian denomination isn't the right cup of tea for each person in this town, there seems to be a greater sense of the working of mysterious forces.

Those forces of mystery are most pronounced in the second volume of the series, *The Witch of Hebron*. Parts of this book look at the lives of two different healers. Dr. Copeland, a man trained in the ways of allopathic medicine, is contrasted against the figure of Barbara Maglie, something of a wise woman and herbalist who lives in the neighboring county of Hebron, the witch referred to in the title. The story also marks out three different flavors of spirituality: Brother Jobe's strict New Faith version of Christianity, the town minister Loren Holder's relaxed Protestantism, and Barbara's free flowing earthy mysticism drawn from magic and folklore. Medicine and mystery interweave among these characters, with Barbara working her powers over Loren to remedy an ailment he had been suffering from, while Dr. Copeland's son Jasper performs an emergency appendectomy on Brother Jobe, saving his life. Nothing is cut and dry; rather, the interplay between the characters and the different world views they each represent

create a rich texture. Each one is a vector and vessel that invisible forces flow through, with their individual personalities acting as filters for those powers.

Brother Jobe is able to tap into these forces as part of his toolkit for navigating a world bedeviled (as he might think) with problems. Besides using his uncanny knack for knowing the secret thoughts of others, he applies his considerable organizational skill towards retrofitting the town's abandoned high school to be reused as the center of operations for his community, turning classrooms into living spaces and workshops. As the series progresses, Jobe and his followers put in a haberdashery and clothing shop in town, rebuild the local tavern, and later on its ruins, a hotel. They also work on a joint operation with Robert Earle and other members of the town council to put in a community laundry operation.

Anytime James Howard Kunstler starts writing about buildings you can tell he is in his element. As a New Urbanist thinker and author of books critiquing suburbia and the way car culture has shaped American communities he is definitely in his element when describing the architectural details, both good and bad, of the buildings the characters inhabit. Most of the cookie cutter homes and McMansions have fallen into severe disrepair by the time the events of the story take place. Nature has had her way with them and they didn't stand the test. Traditional stone buildings and old farmhouses by and large remain. Any renovation or new building had to be accomplished with materials locally sourced and salvaged.

One of the great salvagers of these stories is Andrew Pendergast, a minor character who has a bit more time devoted to him in the third volume, *A History of the Future*. I was quite excited to read a storyline involving him because I was curious about a man who had taken it upon himself to reopen the town library. Andrew is possessed of "diverse skills and interests," so the library is a perfect locus for him. In Union Grove, Andrew plays a number of different roles in the community. None of them were appointed to him, but he took them on because they needed doing. In this the library serves as a symbol of him growing into something of a polymath, or what John Michael Greer might call a Green Wizard—this being someone who has embraced "the task of learning, practicing, and thoroughly mastering a set of mostly forgotten skills to use and share with others." For this reason he is worth focusing on in depth.

Andrew runs the library on limited hours with the help of volunteers. While it is essential work, it doesn't directly put food on the table in a town without a cash economy. Without working computers he has to dust off the card catalog and get that very tactile system of clerical work back into operation. For the citizens of Union Grove, the library becomes a central access point for re-skilling folks who have spent the days before the collapse working in the throw away jobs of the service sector. Having forgotten how to live off the land and the whole slew of tasks associated with running a household economy, they need reliable guides. Thanks to Andrew's efforts these are made available in the form of old books. The knowledge contained in them helps those who seek it save what otherwise might be lost.

Andrew appears to be so alive and full of energy that a man who feels he is broken seeks him out. First this man has the intention of harming Andrew. Then he opens up to the possibility that he could learn something from him. Talking about the state of the world, Andrew tells Jack, "It's up to people to care for other people." This former vagabond ends up staying on in Andrew's home as a kind of servant, but one who is there of his own accord. He works on the chores and projects Andrew gives him in exchange for room and board and for Pendergast's attentiveness towards rehabilitating the man's feeling of brokenness. By teaching him practical skills, Jack begins to walk down a path of recovery, and later in the tale something of a hero.

Besides taking in someone from off the street, one of the ways Andrew shows his care for others is through the establishment of a model garden on his half-acre property. Various towns folk learn to copy him because they have never learned how to grow plants, how to tend food crops, or how to bring in a harvest. Though Kunstler doesn't spell it out, I wouldn't be surprised if some of the townspeople also get some extra seeds off Andrew, as I imagine he's been saving those from season to season. Pendergast also takes to repairing old mechanical clocks. Some anarchist leaning types might not be so disappointed about a world without clocks, or at least time cards. Kunstler, however, imagines a world in which a solution for telling time is still in demand, if at least to keep regular hours at the library.

Andrew isn't just a bookish man and a gardener. During one of the flu epidemics he was responsible for forming the volunteer burial committee. Dr. Copeland had created a makeshift morgue, but when the deaths are so widespread due to massive illness something more immediate had to be done. Rallying the able bodied to the cause, Pendergast led them in the task, and reacquainted his fellow Americans with a part of reality contemporary culture tries very hard to ignore.

He made himself useful to the townsfolk by directing stage shows. With no Netflix or movie theater the meaningful entertainment he created helped bring people together to build morale and a sense of community,

something very different than the isolation of the flat screen. Parallel to this work he led rehearsals for the music circle of the congregational church. In concerts he sat at the piano alongside other musicians, such as Robert Earle on fiddle to play at celebrations on the Fourth of July, Halloween, Christmas, and Easter.

In this character Kunstler foresees a person who works to preserve heritage and humanity in a difficult time. In doing so he adds value to the quality of life of the people around him. This does much to alleviate suffering as the people learn to make do with a standard of living that is markedly different than what the Americans of the late 20th and early 21st centuries believed was a birthright. This listing of Andrew's accomplishments doesn't even exhaust other things Kunstler touches on regarding him.

Another major thread woven through *A History of the Future* is the story of Robert Earle's son Daniel, who has just returned from two years sojourning around America. When he gets back into town, he collapses with exhaustion, illness and the tribulations of the road. It is left up to Dr. Copeland to nurse him back to health. While it is a glorious day for Robert and his girlfriend Britney, it is a day tinged with sadness for Loren Holder and his wife. Their son Evan had taken to the road with Daniel, but he did not come back. As Daniel recovers, he recounts the story of his adventures to his family and to Loren and his wife. The reader is privileged to get the full account in a deftly inserted retrospective narrative.

Daniel and Evan's story takes them on the rivers of New York. This part of the book has the flavor of Americana, with the two young men hitching along the riverside, sleeping along its banks, and seeing how the wider world fares outside of Union Grove. Through Daniel's eyes I was able to glimpse something dear to my heart: travel on the Erie Canal and work being done to reopen the other canal arteries and once again have a low-tech means for transporting goods long distances. A branch of my own ancestral tree had come over from Germany to help build the Miami-Erie canal; they had earned enough money from the intensive manual labor of digging dirt and having it be hauled away by mules that they stopped, bought land and built farms. On a few occasions I'd traveled up to Fort Loramie, Ohio to visit the relatives who still live there, and got to see parts of the Miami-Erie canal that still remain, so I'm always a big fan of seeing stories of the future where writers have put the canals back into working service.

It's not all fun and games though on the Erie. On their travels they meet up with a boatman named Randall McCoy who gives them work as cabin boys and mule drivers on his barge the *Glory*. After paying them a bit of silver coin, wining and dining them, and taking them to houses of ill repute in the newly booming towns along the canal, Randall has pretty well earned their trust. After arriving in Buffalo, Randall tricks the young men into getting a job doing construction work, but when Daniel and Evan go to see the superintendent and ask about the wages they were to earn they realize in a panic that they were press-ganged into work. After a brief struggle, they escape and find their way on a boat traveling Lake Erie, a lake known for its turbulent waters and many shipwrecks. A storm capsizes the boat and Daniel loses Evan to the waters, not knowing if he survived. Daniel continues to travel on his own, and gets himself into a rather sticky situation. Through it, Kunstler is able to show what has happened to the remains of the federal government, and the different nation states the country has begun splitting into.

Daniel starts to heal from his ordeal by the end of the third volume. On his journey he had seen a proliferation of broadsides and circulars being printed with the news and had gotten it into his mind that a newspaper might be something Union Grove could use. After uncovering an old letterpress in the headquarters of Union Grove's abandoned alt weekly, he realizes he just may have a vocation for himself. In the fourth volume, *The Harrows of Spring*, he manages to get it up and running again, with a little help from Andrew Pendergast, who brought books on how to set type and make ink.

Near the beginning of the fourth book there is an incident that shows how humans can be humbled by nature. It isn't an awe-inspiring view of a valley, hills, or forest from the heights of a summit. It's an attack by a bear on Britney on a rickety old bridge where she was crossing the Battenkill River after an afternoon spent gathering wild herbs and fishing for trout. In the new times animals once rare have started making a comeback, bears among them. When the creature caught whiff of the trout it started shambling after her. When she tripped on a disintegrating cross tie the bear lunged and they both fell to the large boulders in the river below. Britney surely would have died if the bear hadn't landed first on its back, snapping its spine. From this initial shock and close encounter with death, Britney goes on to suffer more exquisite traumas that reverberate long after the final pages are closed.

Another major figure in the life of the town is Stephen Bullock, something of a medieval lord presiding over a fiefdom of voluntary peasants. He is one of those guys that might've been called a prepper back in the old times; he saw the general trend and shape of things to come: peak-oil, economic uncertainty, and climate change. That being so, he put the resources he had earned as a lawyer towards the tools that would help him live with comfort and profit, including a hydro-electric generator to provide a modicum of power for his manor—which he used to listen to recordings of Erik Satie. But he is downright teed off when the last of his flywheels break and he doesn't have access to this luxury any longer.

For a time, Stephen serves as magistrate in town, yet his approach to law and punishment is at odds with how the mayor, Brother Jobe, and others think infringements should be handled. Bullock has a martial approach and the men who protect his large farm nail a bandit to a tree. His form of justice is corporal and extends to the use of torture tactics, such as water boarding and clipping off thumbs. Yet for all his harshness Bullock can be a kind and generous man—if a person is willing to live under his strict rules and authority. The many people living in the community of houses and working on his farm do just that and they are rewarded with a decent life. He provides them with food security, shelter, protection, and steady work in a time when such things are scarce. Stephen even rustles up a baseball league. No one has forced them there and he doesn't make them stay if they don't like the way he runs his operation. By having such a large crew to do his bidding, he ends up living large and has a fair amount of political and economic clout throughout the county. Stephen Bullock is someone to be reckoned with.

In this series, James Howard Kunstler has populated a whole town with different characters and shows how they have learned to grow through hardship. When Robert Earle was a software developer he thought nothing of jetting to the west coast for work. Having retooled himself as a carpenter he now lives in a world where each nail and board is precious. The town minister Loren is someone who wrestled with questions of faith, meaning and self worth but finds through his own struggles that he can still be a shepherd to the people in his community. For Andrew Pendergast the new times are exhilarating and come as a breath of freedom. Without his energy being misspent in service to a corporation he is able to roundly develop his many abilities. Daniel Earle returns to Union Grove sick from the trials he endured, but also inspired. After making a full recovery he sets up a business that promises to become profitable to himself while being of service to his fellows.

On the far side of America's ongoing decline there will be many broken institutions and people who also feel they are broken. One thing that can be done as a preventive measure to this tendency is to shore up any existing cracks in your own self. Finding role models to guide thinking and actions is one way to do it, and good fiction can provide good models. Our current society is already under great strain and by seeking to become the kind of individuals who can practice the skills needed for the future now a person can become an example of positive responses to the crises of our times for their family and community.

On our way home from a stroll with our dog, after the fallen tree had been cut and cleared, my wife noticed new silver maple saplings growing in our neighbor's yard. Though they weren't growing right out of the stump of the tree, it still reminded me of the nurse logs so often seen in the rainforests of the Pacific Northwest, a new tree growing on and out of the remains of the old. That's the way Kunstler's town of Union Grove is to me, a town and people growing and gathering their nutrients out of what has fallen. Out of the turbulent past something new and beautiful is being born.

———————————

Read more from Justin Patrick Moore on his website, located at sothismedias.com

Made in the USA
Lexington, KY
25 October 2019